“The brakes aren’t wo

voice was whip tight.

Brielle barely bottled up a scream as they sped through the intersection. A van narrowly missed plowing into Lucas’s side of the car.

“Is there an emergency brake?”

“It might lock the back tires. Too risky.” He pumped the brakes again, but it didn’t decelerate the car. “Hang on.”

Adrenaline burned a trail through Brielle’s veins. The woods blurred, and she gritted her teeth as Lucas fought the momentum of the vehicle. She slammed up against the passenger-side door as they turned to the left.

“There’s a pond right up ahead. I’m going to run us into that to stop. Get ready,” he called out.

He steered the runaway vehicle across the road and into the low shrubs. As soon as the tires hit gravel and plowed into the bushes, their momentum slowed. They bumped and bounced over the rough ground and grass.

Then their car entered the water...

Kerry Johnson has been conversing with fictional characters and devouring books since her childhood in the Connecticut woods. A longtime member of ACFW, she's a seven-time Genesis Contest finalist and two-time winner. Kerry lives on the sunny, stormy west coast of Florida with her engineer husband, two teenage sons, eight-year-old niece and way too many books. She loves long walks, all creatures great and small, and iced chai tea.

Books by Kerry Johnson

Love Inspired Suspense

Snowstorm Sabotage
Tunnel Creek Ambush
Christmas Forest Ambush
Hidden Mountain Secrets

Visit the Author Profile page at LoveInspired.com.

Hidden Mountain Secrets

KERRY JOHNSON

LOVE INSPIRED® SUSPENSE
INSPIRATIONAL ROMANCE

PLEASE RECYCLE • THIS PRODUCT IS RECYCLABLE •

Recycling programs for this product may not exist in your area.

ISBN-13: 978-1-335-59815-8

Hidden Mountain Secrets

For questions and comments about the quality of this book, please contact us at CustomerService@Harlequin.com.

Love Inspired
22 Adelaide St. West, 41st Floor
Toronto, Ontario M5H 4E3, Canada
www.LoveInspired.com

Printed in Lithuania

Lay not up for yourselves treasures upon earth,
where moth and rust doth corrupt, and where
thieves break through and steal: But lay up for
yourselves treasures in heaven, where neither moth
nor rust doth corrupt, and where thieves do not
break through nor steal: For where your treasure is,
there will your heart be also.

—*Matthew* 6:19–21

To the best winter-night snuggle buddy, wedding planner, traveling companion, shopping assistant, crafty aunt and caring sister. Mindy, I'm so thankful God placed us in the same family. Love you.

Acknowledgments

My overflowing gratitude for the trifecta of amazing women who help my books make sense: Kellie, Ali, and my editor, Caroline. The words may be mine, but the story is so much the better because of you all. Thank you.

Jesus. I will follow wherever You lead.

ONE

A crack of thunder shook Brielle Holt's truck as she entered the parking lot of The Antique Depot. Billowing, bruise-colored clouds hung over her store, a one-hundred-year-old red barn, now a lovingly restored antique book and décor shop nestled at the foot of the Blue Ridge Mountains in northwestern South Carolina.

Brielle eyed the only other vehicle in the lot, a blue sedan that was as no-nonsense and reliable as its owner, Shonda, her only full-time employee. She smiled. Even under threat of thunderstorm, Shonda had beat her here this morning. A good thing, too, because their laundry list of to-dos was a mile long, thanks to the influx of books, artwork, and furniture from reclusive millionaire Ronald Gaines's eight-thousand-square-foot mountaintop mansion.

Her smile faded as a chill chased down her arms and legs. Now *deceased* millionaire.

"It's just a big house," she reminded herself. "And those rumors aren't true."

Still, gossip swirled through Tunnel Creek like the BBQ-scented smoke from Marvin's Diner on a Friday night in summer. The sudden death of a wealthy West Coast builder to the stars was fodder for the small-town rumor mill. Added to that were reports of the "Backyard Bandit," a supposed hiker who had broken in through a couple of locals' back doors and stolen items last month. Some said Mr. Gaines had interrupted the Backyard Bandit in action and been killed. Others believed an insider—a family member—had taken him out. Some even claimed he'd ended his own life because of financial and health issues.

A shudder coursed through her as she replayed the heated conversation she'd overheard in the master bedroom suite at the Gaineses' enormous, remote residence yesterday.

"How dare you leave me out of this." A man's sharp voice—Peter Gaines, Ronald's forty-something-year-old son—had cut through the air like a knife, carrying out into the hall.

"Leave *you* out?" a woman shot back. "You're the one who did this."

"All I did was tell the truth, Stella. I had to make a decision."

"No matter how much that decision hurt me." Stella, Mr. Gaines's actress daughter and Peter's younger sister, answered plaintively. "Or Father."

"Don't use Father as a pawn. Just think about what you're doing. Father wouldn't want his collections sold."

Stella had glanced at the doorway and locked eyes with Brielle. Her pixie-like face, framed by short, spiky, white-blonde hair, had crumpled, and her sodden gaze returned to her brother. "Please. I… It hurts too much to keep these things around. I want them gone."

"No, you want the money from selling them," Peter had snarled. Then he noticed Brielle. "What are *you* doing here?"

Brielle had mumbled an apology, then backtracked to the two-story windowed foyer, where her assistant Troy waited with the dolly.

She and Troy had left, returning later that afternoon, after the estate manager and close family friend, Aidan

Donaldson, had given the okay via a text because he wasn't at the mansion that day. Peter and Stella were nowhere to be found the second time, and Ronald Gaines's spacious master suite echoed like a tomb while she and Troy finished loading the marked pieces of furniture, books, and artwork onto the dolly.

Another rumble of thunder brought Brielle's attention back to the present. She kneaded her temples, where a dull headache throbbed.

Peter and Stella were probably stressed about the estate and handling all the details, not to mention upset about their loss. Clearly, they were at odds about selling their father's items. She couldn't help fearing she'd stepped dead center into a family feud.

Raindrops spattered over the hood of her truck. Better get inside. As much as the Gaineses' family argument unnerved her amid the rampant rumors, there was no sense giving more thought to it. She had work to do.

She jumped out of her truck, slammed the door shut, and hurried down the flower-edged walkway toward the store. Two dozen brightly colored gnomes greeted her from their miniature world among her plants and fountain, a favorite of her customers' children. But today, their chubby, grinning faces and the tidy garden village didn't elicit her usual smile.

A flash of movement from the left pulled her gaze from the gnomes to the large utility shed used for overflow items and nicer outdoor furniture. Deer? Coyote? No, the form seemed larger. Human-sized.

She shrank under the store's front awning, her heart pounding. Could it be the Backyard Bandit? What if those rumors *were* true? Goose bumps broke out on her skin. But when she looked back, nothing—no one—was there.

Brielle took a deep breath. Growing up with two older

brothers meant jump-scares were a way of life. Jasper especially liked to appear out of nowhere and pretend to be surprised that he surprised her. It was probably Shonda rearranging items in the shed in order to open up space for the Gaineses' furniture.

She paused and peered at the sign above the front doors. The Antique Depot painted in large, black script letters by her artist mom, Dana Holt, marked the entrance.

For your home away from home, Mom had said with a touch of sadness when she'd gifted it to Brielle. While Mom was proud of Brielle's store and her success, she also made it clear she'd like to see Brielle more often.

Come over anytime, Mom always said on the rare occasions they all got together.

Brielle squared her shoulders and typed in the door code, but the keypad beeped red at her. Twice more she put in the code. Nothing. She frowned down at it and rubbed her damp arms, trying to ward off the chill. Was the battery dying? Couldn't be, she'd just changed it. Wait—it wasn't latched? The door was closed mostly but not latched. That wasn't like Shonda at all. Brielle pushed it all the way open and poked her head inside. A variety of furniture silhouettes along with bookshelf mazes packed the large, darkened front room. No sign of Shonda.

Had Shonda been in such a hurry to beat the rain she hadn't shut the door all the way or turned on the lights? The door locked automatically after two minutes, but since it wasn't completely shut, the bolt hadn't lined up.

"Shonda?" Brielle stepped forward, raising her voice.

No answer.

"Are you here?" Odd. Maybe she was inside the shed.

The backroom door was half-open, and the only light turned on in the entire building illuminated the hallway leading to that storage area. The rest of the store appeared dark. A flurry of prickles rose on her limbs.

Could someone have broken in?

Jasper's recent warning haunted her as she quietly closed the door behind her and warily inched forward. Her police officer brother didn't care for the rural location of her antique store, nearly five miles outside Tunnel Creek, or the fact that she was alone out here some mornings and evenings.

"You need a dog or something. Or a gun."

"I'm not comfortable with them unless it's an 1877 Colt Lightning."

"Not a piece of history. A piece for protection. I don't like you alone out there, especially after these break-ins all over the county."

"Jasper, there's been like three."

"Still," he'd argued. "Better safe than sorry."

Jasper, his son, Gabe, and new wife, Kinsley, along with Brielle's middle brother, Noah, and his fiancée, Lucy, and their mom, Dana, all lived on the other side of Tunnel Creek, right outside Sumter National Forest. While *her* little house sat squarely between her business and town, which meant she was the only outlier in their family.

Something her family mentioned just about every time she finally made it to family gatherings. They wanted to see her more often. She got that, loud and clear. But free time and days off had become sporadic since she'd opened The Antique Depot.

There was always so much to do here.

She shook her head and focused on the present. This was foolish. Shonda was most likely reorganizing, sorting, and tagging items from the Gaines mansion while Brielle stood here, letting rumors unnerve her.

She moved deeper into the store and clicked on the lights.

In the sudden brightness, another pair of eyes clashed with hers. Brielle slapped her palm to her mouth to halt a shriek.

She was staring at *herself* in a full-length window frame mirror.

"It's just a mirror." She blew out a pinched breath, gaping at her widened hazel eyes, damp, wavy brown hair, and the rapid rise and fall of her chest.

Not *just* a mirror. The beautiful bronze patina-finished piece was part of the bedroom suite from Ronald Gaines's master bedroom. Last evening after unloading the items, Troy had unknowingly situated the mirror directly in the line of sight of the front doors.

The urge to locate Shonda lit a fire beneath Brielle's feet. She cut down the center of the store, weaving through the stacked-to-the-brim bookshelves, well-used rocking chairs, two maple chests boasting just about every Hummel statue ever made, tables of vintage kitchen gadgets and pristine dinnerware, and pockets of costume jewelry and crocheted items spread throughout the room. A beautiful little cherry rolltop desk pressed up to a Victorian marble top pub table she'd almost sold yesterday. And chairs. So many chairs. The store was, admittedly, cluttered, but customers seemed to relish the chaos and thrill of stumbling upon something new-to-them.

The more antiques the merrier, Shonda always said. Brielle agreed wholeheartedly.

Brielle stopped short. The crooked French provincial farmhouse table they'd set up by the cash register was pitched forward, the collection of classic children's toys and Little Golden Books on top flung across the floor in a messy heap.

Shonda would never have left these items in this state.

"Shonda? Are you here?" Brielle's voice quavered.

Again, no answer. Only the dissonant ticks of several

grandfather clocks grouped in the corner answered. Brielle dug her cell phone out of her purse. Her fingers shook as she punched in 911. Something wasn't right. And it would take someone at least five or six minutes to get here.

She raised the phone to her ear and held her breath. Reception was often spotty in this area.

Finally, a woman's voice answered. "Nine-one-one, what's your emergency?"

She released the breath. "This is Brielle Holt. I think my store was broken into."

"You're Jasper's sister?"

"Yes. My store is The Antique—"

"I know. I got it, hon." There was a *beep*, then the dispatcher murmured to someone else. A crackle of static, then she came back on the line. "I just notified Jasper. He's on his way. He said to go to your car, get inside, and lock the doors until he arrives."

"But my employee is in here. At least her car is—"

More static crackled in her ear. She pulled the phone away to see if the call was lost. Still connected.

"Please. Tell him to hurry."

She had to get out of here. Get to her car. But what about Shonda? No, she had to do what Jasper said. Brielle whipped around, starting for the front door. But a flash of movement through the front window turned her feet to blocks of ice. Someone clad in black and taller than Shonda.

Her heart crashed into her ribs. Where could she go instead of her car? Maybe she could hide in here. She glanced around, then reached for an iron fire poker. The other fireplace tools clanked together loudly as she yanked the poker loose. If the intruder was out front, going that way wasn't safe. Brielle held her makeshift weapon tightly and slunk around the counter toward the back of her store.

A sharp clatter in the storeroom electrified the air, like

a broom fell over. Was it Shonda? Staring at the storeroom doors, she held the poker out like a medieval sword as her pulse throbbed in her temples.

Brielle edged closer to the storeroom and tried to calm her breathing. What if it was the Backyard Bandit? Her mind immediately went to Ronald Gaines—dead, or murdered?—and a wild shudder weakened her knees.

She stumbled, then righted herself and continued down the short hallway leading to the storeroom, flicking her eyes behind her to the front door. Had it already locked? The automatic lock engaged after two minutes.

Her sense of time felt warped as it sank in that her store was the latest place to be struck by the rumored burglar.

Brielle neared the storeroom door and listened, but only the pounding of her heartbeat filled her ears. Stacked boxes containing dishes and glassware lined the employee-only area, still needing to be priced and tagged. Her arm quivered under the weight of the gritty iron poker. She peeked into the back room, observing the worktables lining the edges of the room and a dozen imposing pieces of furniture as well as tall bookcases clustered in the middle.

Things appeared as they had last night when she'd closed up.

But where was Shonda?

She opened the door wider, inching inside, and a gasp lodged in her throat.

A still form lay across a leather ottoman in the middle of the furniture. Brielle's stomach plummeted as she catalogued the details. Shoulder-length, dark hair. Tie-dyed Crocs Shonda often wore to work, socks peeking out from beneath.

"Shonda?"

She crept closer, her muscles painfully tense and nausea rising in her throat. A loud *whoosh* of air warned her that something—*someone*—was rushing at her. Powerful arms wrapped around her from behind, and the glint of a knife shone brightly from the corner of her eye. The pungent scent of body odor and a strange, musky smell burned her nose. Brielle screamed, jabbing her elbow at him and wriggling away. Her attacker grabbed her purse strap before she got too far and yanked her back. She ducked so the purse strap shifted over her shoulder and head, escaping its hold. Then she pivoted and lifted the poker high, jabbing it forward as hard as she could at the man. It *thunked* into her attacker's midsection, and the knife clattered to the ground.

Brielle shrieked as their combined momentum sent her flying into Ronald Gaines's mahogany armoire. She held her grip on the poker as she bounced off the wood wardrobe and spun, landing hard against the leather ottoman. She rolled over Shonda's limp form, and then hit the ground with a solid *thud.*

Pain crisscrossed her back and shoulders, releasing sharp tremors through her arms and legs. *Please, God...*

Her pitiful prayer was cut off at the undeniable sound of the man rising to his feet and kicking aside the cocktail table in his way.

"Stay away from me!" She kept the poker raised in front of her, and her legs wobbled like a newborn fawn's as she tried to stand. They gave way, and she faced him from her knees, poker held out in warning. She was cornered. No place to go.

Please, God, she prayed again, remembering what she'd tried so hard to forget from her childhood. *God is your strong tower and fortress of protection*, her dad had told her many times as a child at the school where her parents worked as missionaries in Cameroon. She repeated the verse now, the words like armor over her heaving chest.

Staring up, Brielle took in the black mask hiding most of her assailant's face. All she could make out were dark brown eyes and sneering lips curled over straight white teeth.

He came at her, and she swung the poker with two hands and all the strength she had in her. The man ducked away, but the iron nicked the side of his head hard enough that he let out an ear-scalding oath.

The howl of sirens resonated through the room like a hallelujah. *The police.* Jasper.

"This isn't finished." Her attacker pushed past her with a frustrated growl, shoving her back down beside the ottoman and Shonda.

She landed at an awkward angle on the poker and something else sharp. *The knife.* Pain shot like lightning through her side, making her gasp. She focused on the sound of the attacker flinging open the back door and the resounding smack as it slammed shut seconds later.

He was gone. Still, her chest tightened as though she wore an eighteenth-century corset. Curling her knees to her middle, she tried to draw in a breath, but her lungs felt like deflated balloons. The invisible laces were tightening… tightening…until it was impossible to draw in more air.

Brielle rolled onto her back, gulping in shallow breaths like a beached fish, faster and faster, picturing Shonda's dark hair spread across the leather length of the ottoman, obscuring her sweet face.

"Shonnie…" A strangled sob lodged in her throat. She pressed a fist to her chest, willing away the tightness so she could draw breath.

This isn't finished, the man had said. Would he come back? Stars dotted Brielle's vision, tiny sparks that merged into a solid screen behind her eyes as she succumbed to the darkness.

"There he goes." Lucas Scott pointed at the masked man darting out from the back of Brielle Holt's store and tearing into the woods behind it.

His longtime friend—and Brielle's older brother—Officer Jasper Holt floored his squad car's gas pedal as they rounded the bend to Brielle's store.

"Description?" Jasper barked.

"Five-ten to five-eleven, one-eighty-five. Wearing a black mask, dark clothes."

Jasper radioed in what Lucas saw, then took a sharp left into the antique store parking lot. The vehicle splashed through a puddle as Jasper slammed into Park.

Lucas leapt out and ran to Brielle's truck. "She's not in here." He sprinted up the walkway, his Glock unholstered and ready. Jasper unloaded Dash, his K9 partner, as Lucas checked the front doors. Locked. He wiped the rain from his eyes, then started around the right side of the building.

"Going right," Lucas called out.

"Got it. I'm going left," Jasper answered.

Mud squelched beneath Lucas's boots, and the heavy gray clouds overhead released a drenching rain that made it difficult to follow tracks.

They arrived at the back doors at the same time, and Jasper signaled for Lucas to go inside the store, while Jasper and Dash's job was to chase down the perp. As a CSI with SLED, the South Carolina Law Enforcement Division, Lucas was trained to process crime scenes.

Lucas pictured Brielle Holt's large hazel eyes and her friendly grin, and his gut churned. Why wasn't she waiting in the car where she was supposed to be?

Had they made it in time?

Jasper signaled Dash. The Dutch shepherd's head cocked, then Jasper unhooked his leash and spoke to him. Dash shot into the woods like a canine bullet, and Jasper followed at a fast run. They would track—and hopefully catch—the criminal while Lucas investigated the store.

Lucas approached the back doors quietly, listening for

several seconds. Only the *tap-tap* of raindrops falling from the roof to the sidewalk filled the silence.

Then he gripped the doorknob and called out, "This is Special Agent Lucas Scott. Come out now with your hands up." He waited to the count of five, then burst through the door, weapon aimed, his gaze swinging back and forth across the large, crowded space. Bulky dressers, a long dining room table with chairs, a few boxes, and a dark brown leather sofa were packed into what must be a storage room.

An ideal location for a criminal to hide.

He repeated the warning in case there was a second suspect. No movement.

"Brielle? Are you here?"

Lucas checked the outside corners of the room then rushed forward to scour in between the furniture. He avoided touching anything in case there were any prints, hair, or blood that would identify the criminal.

His scalp itched as he veered between the dressers and a table. Then he froze. *There.*

A woman lay prone. Dark, shoulder-length hair fanned out, obscuring her face. An invisible hand clutched his windpipe.

Blood pooled beneath her middle. Knife wound? Lucas's own stomach clenched into a painful knot. He'd seen all shades of brutal human nature working as a crime scene investigator for SLED and, before that, as a police officer. But this…horrible memories swarmed him like flies on death. *Leah.*

He punched the spare waist radio Jasper had flung at him on their way over here and forced air into his vocal cords. "Get an ambulance out here. *Now.*"

The call would distract Jasper on his search, but it had to be done.

He holstered his gun, crouched near her body, and flipped open the individual first aid kit strapped to his belt. Lucas grasped the large bandage from the IFAK and applied pressure to the wound on her abdomen.

He'd spent the last few years hardening his heart toward these types of scenes. Humankind was capable of great good, but also too much evil. As the Bible warned, the love of many had grown cold. He and Jasper had been friends since their days at Tunnel Creek High. Jasper, Noah, and Lucas had gone fishing together in school, played ball, studied for finals, and had each other's backs. Jasper had been there for him when Leah, his fiancée, was kidnapped and found murdered near Greenville years back.

Lucas's shoulders felt like hundred-pound weights sat on them as he reached his free hand to gently move her hair away from her face.

He straightened. This wasn't Brielle! This must be her coworker. The two women resembled each other in hair color and general build.

Then where was Brielle?

Someone moaned.

"Brielle?" He called out.

"Lucas?" Her voice sounded weak but close by.

He kept pressure on the wound and carefully leaned over the injured woman. Brielle Holt lay on the floor on the other side of the ottoman, her arms curled over her torso. Blinking groggily.

"Brielle? Who— What happened?" Her brown hair haloed her pale face, tears tracked down her cheeks, and her chest rose and fell with shallow, uneven breaths. "It's okay. You're safe. Slow your breathing. There you go. Inhale. Slow exhale. Good. Is this your coworker?"

She struggled upright, using her hands to brace herself. "Yes. Shonda Barkley. She got here before me. Is she okay?" Brielle's watery gaze followed him as he checked the bandage covering Shonda's wound.

"She's alive. The ambulance is on its way. What about you? Do you have any injuries?"

"I don't think so. I—"

The back door slapped into the wall as Jasper burst into the room, Dash at his side. "Where is she? Brielle?"

"Jasper, hold up." Lucas held out a hand. "Brielle is here. She's okay. Her coworker is injured. I need you to keep Dash back. This is a crime scene."

Jasper's frantic gaze jumped from the wounded woman to Brielle. "That's Shonda?"

"Affirmative." Lucas replaced the bloody bandage with fresh gauze.

Jasper spoke to Dash, and the dog sank to his haunches. Then he called in the situation, his voice taut with anger. The dispatcher reassured them the ambulance was on the way even as sirens sounded in the distance.

"Thanks. We hear them." Jasper disconnected the call then weaved through the furniture until he reached his sister's side. "I'm here, sis."

He lifted Brielle up, then wrapped her in a tight embrace. Brielle sobbed quietly in his arms.

"I'm so glad you're okay," Jasper muttered into her hair.

Lucas looked away when Jasper dashed a hand across his cheek. He'd always loved the Holt family, and more than ever he was moved by their familial bond.

"I should've listened to you, Jasper." Brielle sniffled into his chest. "Shonda is hurt because—"

"This isn't your fault," Lucas interrupted. "The responsibility lies solely with the criminal who broke into your store and did this."

Doors slammed outside. Moments later, the EMTs rushed in. Jasper, Brielle, and Lucas stepped out of their way. The medical technicians loaded Shonda onto a stretcher and exited the crowded storage room with bustling efficiency.

Lucas peered at the space where Brielle had fallen, noting the knife on the floor.

"I need evidence bags so I can get to work." He pushed his glasses up on his nose, then caught her eye as she pulled away from Jasper. "Is there anything else I should be aware of here?"

"My purse is over there. Can I get it?" She pointed to the doorway Lucas assumed led to the main part of the antique store.

"Did your attacker touch it at all?" Lucas asked.

"He grabbed the strap to pull me closer," she recalled. "But I'm not sure if he touched the inside."

"For now, leave it. Might have prints on it."

"You're bleeding," Jasper said, studying a quarter-sized spot of blood saturating her shirt.

She touched the spot and winced. "The knife poked me when I landed on the floor. It's not that bad."

"I'll be the judge of that," Jasper said.

Lucas averted his eyes as Jasper and Brielle inspected the wound on her side. He swept the room, taking in the crime scene. Looking for dirt, scraps of clothing, lint. If only he'd brought the DSLR camera, but it was in his parents' condo in Tunnel Creek.

For now, his cell would have to do. He snapped a few pictures, then turned to the siblings.

Jasper addressed his sister. "It may not be bad, but you're still going to the hospital."

He and Jasper bookended Brielle and helped her through the doors. Once they were outside, Jasper tugged a ragged stuffed animal from his back pocket, tossing it to Dash. His reward for good behavior. The dog clamped it tightly in his powerful jaws, shaking his head side to side as though making sure the old thing was dead. Lucas almost smiled.

"Lucas," Brielle asked, pulling his attention from the K9.

"I can't believe you're here. What are you doing back in Tunnel Creek?"

"Checking on my parents' place. They're in Europe for ten days." He glanced at Jasper. "We met up this morning, and when we found out you needed help, I came along."

"I couldn't believe it when I heard your voice. Are you still living in Myrtle Beach?"

"I am." The Tunnel Creek Police Department wasn't large enough to have their own crime scene department, which was why he'd been put on special assignment by his department head to investigate Ronald Gaines's suspicious death.

As they led Brielle to the ambulance, Lucas scowled at the ground. The storm had passed, leaving behind mud puddles and wet grass. A mess outside as well as inside. Which would work against them for tracking the criminal and for tread analysis.

"What happened when you and Dash were in the woods?" Lucas asked Jasper.

"We chased the suspect up to Sixty-Four, about a quarter mile. There's a single-lane side road, Penny Lane. The perp must've parked his truck there. By the time Dash and I got to the road, he had driven off. Headed east. I notified Chief McCoy. There's an APB out."

"Did you get a look at the vehicle?"

"Not a great one. Dark blue, Chevy maybe. Used."

Lucas gave a single nod. Lord willing there were small details—fingerprints, hair, fibers of clothing, even blood—that would help identify the suspect. He counted on those tiny markers to point him and the officers in the right direction.

Another officer arrived, along with a second ambulance. When the man hopped out of his squad car, Jasper motioned his colleague over. "Matt, this is Lucas Scott with SLED. Lucas, Matt Reed. Lucas lives in Myrtle Beach, works in the crime scene department." He briefly explained what happened while the EMTs attended to Brielle's injury. "Shonda Barkley was just taken to the hospital. Knife wound, possible head injury."

"Got it. I'll get the crime scene contained, then take Brielle's statement." Matt Reed jogged around to the antique store's back doors.

Lucas propped a hip against Jasper's squad car.

Jasper fixed Lucas with an intent stare. "I know you'll be busy with the Gaines investigation, but I sure could use your help on this one." He leaned in close. "I'm wondering if the two crimes are related, to be perfectly honest."

Lucas cocked his head. "You're thinking this was the Backyard Bandit?"

"I don't want to automatically jump to that conclusion," Jasper answered with measured words. "But if it's black and yellow and buzzes around flowers, it can probably sting you. With your permission, I'd like to call Chief McCoy and make sure we can get you on as special counsel to this case."

"I'm already on extended jurisdiction to investigate the Gaines case. This shouldn't be a problem." Lucas's mind churned. "I'd like to secure Ms. Barkley's cell phone and personal items to check her contacts, recent calls and texts."

"I'll get Matt on that right away."

"What about security cameras?" Lucas hadn't noticed any around back.

"Only one, in the front." Jasper pointed toward the antique store's front awning. "I've been telling her she needs at least two more and some inside as well."

"Hmm. We'll check that one then." Lucas snapped his fingers. "Remind the officers to be cautious inside, please. I still need to secure the core area. It was difficult to narrow down with all that large furniture."

"You got it." Jasper tapped his utility belt twice then addressed Brielle, who had finished up with the EMTs and was approaching them. "I'm going back inside. Can you stay here with Lucas for a minute?"

She nodded mutely at him.

He tweaked her arm. "I love you, sis."

"Love you, too. Thank you for coming for me." Her gaze swung from Jasper to Lucas. "Both of you."

"We'll catch this guy." Jasper nodded once, then set off into the store.

Brielle wandered closer to Lucas. He'd always had a keen sense of smell, probably due to his chef mother and being raised around cooking, food, and all the unique seasonings that came along with that, and Brielle smelled like oranges and cedar. She was sunny dispositioned as well as strong, so the scent seemed appropriate.

He shook off the odd thought and turned to her. "Not exactly the way you wanted to start your day."

"No." Her posture sagged. "I can't believe this happened. At my store. Have you heard of the Backyard Bandit?"

He nodded slowly. "I have, but I don't want to jump to any conclusions. It's too early to know anything for certain."

"True." She exhaled softly. "I keep thinking, what if I'd gotten here later..."

"I advise against the 'what-ifs.' I'm grateful—we're all grateful—you're safe. We'll pray Ms. Barkley is okay."

"Lucas." She straightened. "I just remembered something else. The man who attacked us said, 'I'll finish this' or 'this isn't finished,' when he heard the sirens, before he ran off."

Lucas kept his features impassive at this disconcerting news. "Make sure you share that with Officer Reed when you give your statement."

"I will." She rubbed her eyes. "I hope I remember all these details. I still feel like my brain is working in slow motion."

"You're in shock. That's normal."

She huffed. "None of this is normal."

"Unfortunately, in my world, it is."

"That sounds awful." She edged closer to him, pressing her warm arm to his. Comforting him when he should be comforting her. "I hope it's not always that way for you."

"Not always." He tried to inject some optimism into his voice. But working crime scenes, there was no debating that he was faced with the worst symptoms of the fall. With the underbelly of society and broken humanity.

"What if Shonda doesn't make it?" Brielle hunched sideways, resting her head on his shoulder.

His muscles tensed, then relaxed at the needed connection. He'd always appreciated Brielle's sweet, quirky personality and their mutual love of books and reading. They'd frequently exchanged their favorite books in high school. He'd looked forward to seeing the story through her eyes, and she'd been a trooper about reading the sci-fi classics he enjoyed.

The last they'd seen each other was at Jasper and Kinsley's wedding, though it had been brief and too loud of a setting to do much catching up. They'd had little contact other than emails and book recommendations since he'd moved away and attended college in Charleston. After that he'd accepted his first position with the police department in Myrtle Beach, then earned his master's degree in criminal justice before joining the crime scene department with SLED.

Lucas gently set his chin on her hair. His best friend's little sister was hurting. Scared. Worried. What could he say to her?

"'I will never leave you nor forsake you,'" Lucas quoted Joshua 1:5. The same words his mom had told him when he was angry and in pieces after Leah's murder. "No matter what, God is with us. We're never, ever abandoned. Got it?"

"If you say so."

"It's true. And we can pray that she makes it."

She released a long sigh. "I've felt so far from God for so long, I don't know if I can."

"Because of what happened with your dad overseas?"

She hesitated for several heartbeats. "Yes."

"Then I'll have faith for you until yours is stronger."

Jasper jogged out of the antique store and headed their way. Brielle pulled away and slipped into her brother's arms.

"Lucas, there's no sign of Ms. Barkley's cell phone. It wasn't on her person, either. No sign of her purse." Jasper addressed Brielle. "Do you know where she kept it?"

"In a filing cabinet in the back room. The cabinet is gray, with three drawers. We kept personal items in the bottom drawer. Speaking of, when do I get my purse back? Cell?"

"I'll return those as soon as they're cleared for prints," Lucas said.

"Good," Jasper said. "Once you check out the crime scene, see if Shonda's purse and cell phone turn up. Also, let's take a look in her car. If not, we can assume the suspect took it or it's at her apartment. I'll send an officer there to check things out. Brielle will be riding to the hospital, and I'll follow her there."

"In the ambulance, Jasper? Is that necessary?"

"Yes, and yes. You'll also have to give Matt your statement before we go." Jasper turned to Lucas. "Do you need anything else?"

"Evidence bags. Gloves." Lucas rattled off a few more items. "That should do it for now."

Jasper, Brielle, and Lucas made their way to Jasper's squad car. Jasper tugged out one of the boxes from the trunk, then handed it to Lucas. "Here. First aid kit. Gloves and evidence bags are inside. Matt will be here if there's something else that comes up."

"I have a spare truck key in the drawer under the cash register," Brielle told Lucas. "You can drive my truck back into town, if that's okay."

"That would be helpful. Thanks." Lucas flipped quickly through the box Jasper handed him. "Looks like I'm all set."

"Call or text if anything else comes up. Otherwise, I'll check in shortly." Jasper reached out one of his long arms, arms that had been nearly impossible to get past in basketball, and clutched Lucas in a rough side embrace. "Thanks for this, man. I owe you."

"You don't owe me anything. I'm grateful she's safe, and I'll do my best."

"I don't doubt it."

Jasper and Brielle started toward Officer Reed.

"Hey, Brielle," Lucas called out. "Don't forget to mention what the perp said to you before he ran off."

"I will." She waved.

Lucas waved back, then strode around the side of the antique store. He considered the case with a scowl. Before this, he'd been loath to believe the rumors of the Backyard Bandit, especially in relation to Ronald Gaines's death. Now, he wasn't so sure they were rumors. The Backyard Bandit's MO was burglarizing houses. So why had Brielle's antique store been chosen by this elusive local thief? Or was there something else to this brutal attack?

Had Brielle and her coworker been targeted? Brielle had wondered aloud minutes ago what would've happened to Shonda if she had arrived any later. But Lucas's mind followed that mental rabbit trail to a realization that sent his pulse into overdrive.

If he and Jasper had arrived any later, Brielle would most likely be as badly off as Shonda Barkley…or worse.

TWO

Lucas stepped into the elevator and hit the button for the hospital's third floor. He'd spent a few hours processing the crime scene and brought the evidence bags to the station to tag the items he'd secured from the scene, including the video camera above the store's front door. Unfortunately, it appeared the attacker had used a rock or other hard object to crush the lens. He'd take a look at that later. After logging the items he'd bagged on an extra computer set up in Jasper's office, he sent them on to the closest crime lab, in Greenville. Then he'd spoken to the doctors about Shonda Barkley's wounds.

Brielle's coworker had sustained a knife wound to her stomach, but worse, a traumatic brain injury. From the placement of the furniture, Lucas surmised that she'd struck her head on the oak dresser then landed on the ottoman. That would explain the swelling on her brain. There would be no questioning Ms. Barkley; at least not yet. Lord willing, she would be okay once she healed. But for now, Brielle's testimony alone, plus the items found at the scene, would have to guide him and the police officers on the case.

His stomach twisted from the turkey ranch wrap he'd wolfed down on the way over from the station. Jasper had updated him about Brielle via text. They'd cleaned her wound and bandaged it, but stitches weren't required. She would be released late afternoon or early evening, once her CT scan came back. Jasper asked if Lucas would mind accompanying Brielle back to her house so he could go home to be with his very-pregnant wife, Kinsley.

Lucas adjusted the black messenger bag slung over his shoulder as he considered the crime scene. It didn't appear anything was stolen. Though it wasn't easy to tell in such a packed store. The overturned table in front of the cash register was likely the result of Ms. Barkley running away from the attacker and trying to stop him. Every penny of the six-hundred-and-fifty-five dollars in the cash register remained untouched. And then there were the perp's own words.

This isn't finished.

After Leah's death, he'd perfected an emotionless response to the various gruesome scenes he'd been exposed to over the last few years. But when someone he knew was in danger, threatened, or hurt…like his best friend's little sister…

Something dark turned around inside him. A rage-driven hatred that he knew wasn't from the Lord. One that had no place in his life. He'd fought that darkness for years after Leah was killed, and he couldn't allow it to gain a foothold in his heart now.

The elevator dinged then opened, the noxious lemony scent of Clorox and rubber gloves hitting his nose hard. He followed the numbers to Brielle's room. Jasper's booming voice carried into the hallway, along with their mom's, Dana Holt.

Lucas stepped inside and set the messenger bag in the corner. "You really should find a volume button, Jasper."

"Lucas." Dana clasped her hands, then hurried across the room, wrapping him in a metallic-scented hug. Her color-flecked, gray-threaded brown hair tickled his nose.

Always the paint smell. But it was part of who she was, and he loved her for it.

"Jasper said you saved Brielle's life." She squeezed until his ribs ached. "Thank you."

"I don't know about that. Brielle took care of herself until we got there."

"Yes, well, she's always been good at that." Dana Holt released him and stepped back, her burdened gaze flickering toward Brielle. His smile flipped upside down. Years ago, Jasper had shared that Dana and Brielle seemed to be on two very different wavelengths. That his mom and sister circled around each other warily, and it bothered Jasper because he didn't understand why the distance between them or what had happened.

"Quit being humble. You saved her." Jasper came over and smacked Lucas's shoulder. "In a way."

"It was a coincidence." He playfully pushed Jasper away, then met Brielle's eyes. "How's the patient holding up?"

She sat in a chair beside the window, her thick brown hair knotted on top of her head and her skin paler than it should be. She sent him a thumbs-up.

"What coincidence?" Dana returned to her daughter's side near the window.

"If Lucas hadn't forgotten something at his parents' condo and then said he had to go get it before we went out to the mine, today could've been a different story," Jasper explained. "I wanted to go straight to the welcome center to investigate last night's vandalism, but Lucas said he *had* to go back to his parents' condo."

"It's not a big deal." Heat climbed Lucas's neck as all the eyes in the room swung to him.

Jasper continued like Lucas hadn't spoken. "We had just left his parents' condo when Brielle's nine-one-one call came in." Jasper's throat bobbed on a long swallow, and his joking demeanor morphed into seriousness. "If I'd had my way, we would've been on the opposite side of town, twenty minutes away, when the call came in. Matt Reed was on duty, too, but he was up at Whisper Mountain Tunnel for a fender bender."

"So, you would've taken a lot longer to get to my store if you hadn't gone back to Lucas's parents' place." Brielle connected the dots.

Jasper nodded.

"Thank You, Lord, for Your intervention." Dana patted her daughter's shoulder, and Brielle offered a weak smile in return.

"What did you want so badly from your parents' place?" Brielle's gaze drilled a hole through his head.

Lucas groaned. This was getting out of hand. "I, ah, I forgot a book I wanted to give you. For your birthday." He shrugged. "I was in a hurry to meet Jasper and I left it on the kitchen counter. Jasper said we might head over to your store later today."

"A book saved me? Is it an old book?"

"The story is old, but the book is new." He put his palms up in an *I surrender* gesture. "Best I can do."

"So yeah, we owe Lucas and his nerdiness for saving you." Jasper punched his arm again. "Do you mind if we get going? I'm starving and I miss my wife and son."

"Not at all. I'm here for the long haul." Lucas pulled off his glasses and rubbed the bridge of his nose. "How is Gabe handling the idea of a sibling?"

"Great. He has requested that we name the baby Flower if she's a girl or Optimus Prime if it's a boy."

Lucas set his glasses back on his nose and chuckled. "Still into Transformers, I see."

"I would stay, but I have an art class to teach tonight," Dana piped up. "I promised Bev I would cover for her tonight at the senior center. Acrylics," she said by way of explanation. "Do you need anything to eat, Lucas?"

"I grabbed food on the way here, thanks."

Dana slowed on her way out of the room. "You're sure you don't mind taking her home once she's discharged?"

"It's not a problem. I'm here to help."

"Noah is working an overnight camping event with a Boy Scout troop in the Ellicott Rock Wilderness area, or else he'd help out tonight," Dana shared.

"Poor Noah. It's not a problem at all to hang out now and stay at her place tonight."

"Take it easy, please," Jasper said to Brielle, then met Lucas's eye. "Thanks again. I wouldn't trust anyone else to do this." He followed his mom out into the hallway, leaving Lucas and Brielle alone.

"Why do men have to beat each other up to show affection?"

He sank into the chair near the door. "It allows us to show our gratitude and still feel masculine at the same time. Plus, it feels good to punch something alive every now and then."

"And do you feel like punching people very often?"

"When you spend your days in my line of work, the urge crosses the mind often."

"Oh, right." Her brows dipped in sympathy. "Well, at the moment you look too tired to punch anything."

"I am." He reclined in the chair and closed his eyes for a moment.

"You don't have to stay."

"You can't get rid of me that easily." He opened his eyes to find her watching him. "You really shouldn't be alone right now."

"Jasper said that about a dozen times. The doctor doesn't think I have a concussion."

"I hope he's right. It's best to confirm that with the CT scan results."

"Right." She shivered. "Hopefully we get them soon."

He stood, grabbed a tan blanket from the foot of the hospital bed, and stepped over to wrap it around her shoulders.

A lovely smile lit up her face as she curled her fingers into the blanket. "Thanks."

"Are you up for answering some questions?"

"I can try to, but I think my answers will be all over the place. My brain feels like oatmeal."

"Let's endeavor to try."

"You always did like those fancy words."

He dug his cell from his pocket. "*Endeavor* is a fancy word?"

"*I* don't use it." She held the blanket with one fist, then shook her hair out of the knot on the top of her head. She'd always been pretty in a subtle and natural way. Now, nearly fifteen years after he first met her, he couldn't deny she'd matured into that beauty. It shone from the inside out.

If he hadn't known her before, she would've caught his eye and his attention. The acknowledgment felt like he'd touched a light socket with a wet finger.

Lucas ground his back teeth. Speaking of teeth, Jasper would knock Lucas's out if he caught wind of these types of thoughts toward his sister. Jasper had just said Lucas was the only guy he trusted to stay at his sister's place overnight—he needed to live up to that expectation.

One summer afternoon during high school, Brielle had—out of the blue—asked if he wanted to go to homecoming with her the next year. They were all out fishing, he and Jasper and Noah, and Lucas had just started noticing Leah, who was in his grade. Lucas had thought Brielle was joking, but later, she'd seemed distant. Now he wondered if he'd hurt Brielle that day, and he winced at the realization he probably had.

His seventeen-year-old self's observational skills were obviously lacking. And if she'd harbored any feelings toward him back then, surely they were long gone after what he'd allowed to happen with Leah.

But that was all in the past now.

"So, let's go through this morning one more time." He adjusted his glasses then leaned forward, resting his elbows on his knees. "If you find this too difficult, we can postpone it until tomorrow."

"I'll try. But wait, aren't you on vacation? How are your parents?"

"Distracting me?" He sent her a teasing smile. He wasn't actually in Tunnel Creek on vacation, but hesitated to talk about the investigation into Ronald Gaines's death. "My parents are probably in a castle right now as we speak, eating bonbons and gazing out at green pastures."

"That sounds wonderful."

He chuckled. "You still like castles, huh?"

"Of course. They're full of old things."

"Ah. Right. Now it makes sense. Antiques." He shook off the lightheartedness and pinned her with a pointed look. "Speaking of antiques. I spent a few hours at your store today, going over the crime scene. Shonda isn't currently able to help us with this investigation." He paused. "Which means I need *your* help. You saw this guy. I didn't. I need to know what you saw, what you heard, even what you smelled when you walked into your store this morning."

Brielle held Lucas's bright blue gaze. His striking eyes had gained a few creases at the corners through the years, but his wire-rimmed glasses, wet-sand-colored short hair, and trimmed beard were the same as the last time she saw him, at Jasper and Kinsley's wedding. They'd greeted each other and tried to catch up at the rehearsal dinner and then on the wedding day, but there was so much to do, their conversation hadn't gotten far before they were each called away for other duties.

Jasper had occasionally mentioned how Lucas was doing through the years.

Once, she'd harbored a teenage infatuation with her eldest brother's kind, soft-spoken, smart best friend. Not to mention cute. But Lucas made it clear he wasn't interested, that he only viewed her as Jasper's sister. She cringed a little now, recalling that fishing trip to the grist mill lake, when she'd tagged along and made a fool of herself by requesting he teach her to bait a hook, then asking if he would go to homecoming with her.

She'd been well aware of how to fish for fish, just not how to fish for a *boy* she had a crush on. Warmth bloomed on her cheeks, and she stared down at her hands.

Soon after, he and Leah began dating. Lucas might've teased her and asked with sincerity about her art projects and books she'd read, but only ever as a friend. That was it.

She lifted her chin. "Wait, did you ask what I *smelled* during the attack?"

"Yes. Any and all details like that are helpful." He held out his cell phone with the recording app ready to go, along with a notebook and pen on one folded leg. "Your mom paints canvases. I paint pictures of crimes and how they happened."

She twisted her mouth in thought. "When I first got there, I noticed Shonda's car. It was parked in the usual spot. I ran up to the front door to get out of the rain and found the door closed but not latched, which was highly unusual."

"She always shut it," he prompted.

"Always. We kept the store locked completely or else

people would walk in, want to shop. We do have a sign that says when we're closed or open, but an open door is enough invitation for some very determined customers."

"Understandable. And there's a code for this door? Who knows the code?"

"Me and Shonda, obviously. Troy, my part-time help, Jasper, my mom..." Her mind stretched. "My friend Lindsey because she and her daughter help organize items sometimes."

He made a note. "Go on."

Brielle recounted the state of her store. The mirror, darkness, and the new items from the Gaines mansion. The turned-over table near the cash register. How the storeroom looked about the same as last night, except for...she wilted. Except for her friend laying on the ottoman.

"Any other details that stand out to you? Smells, sounds?"

"Now that you say that, there was a strange smell. It was the man. He had body odor but he also wore a really strong cologne. It was woodsy and musky and just, yuck." She grimaced.

"Have you ever smelled it before?" His gaze intensified.

"Maybe? But definitely not often."

"I'll look into that, try to get you samples. I also checked the camera you have set up over the front door. It's damaged. Looks like a rock or hard object was used to smash the lens. I noticed it's a Blink camera. How do you check the videos?"

"There's an app on my cell, but—" she sank lower "—I rarely check it."

"I'll need to take a look."

She shared her phone code, and he wrote it down. "Why would someone come after Shonda? She's a kind, helpful woman. I can't imagine she has any enemies."

"I don't know the whys yet." He dragged a hand through

his hair. “Criminals don’t always have motives, unfortunately. My gut tells me he was focused on one of you or something in your store.” He peered at her so intently her heart turned over. “Could he have been coming after one of the items from the Gaines mansion?”

“It’s possible.”

“Do you have a market value for the items you took from the mansion?”

She mentally skipped back over the load, adding up the items with rough estimates. “Altogether, what we brought over was worth maybe fifteen to twenty grand. But we—I mean *I*—haven’t valued them officially yet.”

Lucas’s mouth curved down in thought.

“Do you think he tried to kill Shonda over that stuff?” She shook her head. “It doesn’t make sense.”

“When Leah was murdered, I was mad. Mad at the man who did it, mad at God. Mad at myself for not stopping it. I tried desperately to make sense of it, but it didn’t *make* sense, and unfortunately never will.”

“I’m sorry, Lucas. You were so young and that was… so awful.”

His chest hitched. “I was certain a good God wouldn’t allow this. Leah wanted to teach, to be a mother. Why had God stopped that?” Lucas squinted down at his phone when it pinged. “But as time passed, and I thawed toward the Lord, He showed me that He was still good. He showed me circumstances where He did protect His people. That despite the state of this broken world, He is there, with us. But no doubt about it, there are things I’ve seen…”

“Worse than fiction?”

“Much worse than fiction. Hold up.” He read whatever text came over his cell screen, his brow furrowed.

“What is it?” She shivered despite the blanket he’d handed her.

"Jasper forwarded the report from the lab. The prints from the scene match a Theodore Hardwick. Born in Las Vegas. Early forties, had two misdemeanors in his twenties. Drunk driving and trespassing. They've put an APB out for him."

Trespassing? "Do you think he could be the Backyard Bandit?"

"It's possible. But, if so, the innocuous beginning to his local crime spree—breaking in through the back door and stealing small items—clearly didn't satiate him." Lucas set his cell down. "Here's what bothers me, and what I want to go over with you. From your accounts and from what I saw, the attacker barely touched any of the items in your store. No prints on the cash register. Now, maybe it was because you arrived and he didn't get the chance to. But he could've broken in earlier this morning, when you all weren't there. It's almost like he didn't want the cash and wasn't interested in stealing any material items."

"Right." She curled the blanket tighter around her shoulders. "But why?"

"The million-dollar question. Jasper checked Shonda's file. It came back clean, no arrests. Only one speeding ticket, and that was twenty years ago." His blue eyes locked on her. "After what the suspect said to you, I'm starting to surmise that this was possibly a targeted, even personal attack. Like he was after Shonda…or you, specifically." His brow furrowed again.

Peter Gaines's furious expression the other night burst into her mind like Fourth of July fireworks. "Lucas, don't be mad."

He straightened. "What is it?"

"I forgot that yesterday there was an incident at the Gaines mansion."

"What incident?"

"I overheard an argument between Stella and Peter Gaines in the master bedroom. Peter was angry about Stella wanting to sell their father's things. Then they…blamed each other for something. It was pretty heated, and when they saw me, they stopped speaking. Peter asked what I was doing there."

He scribbled more notes. "Then what happened?"

She relayed what she'd heard. "Troy and I left. Later I checked with Aidan Donaldson. Aidan is the estate manager for Ronald Gaines and, he says, an old family friend. He lives part-time at the mansion. I called him because he's in charge of the estate and I was worried they'd changed their minds. But he told me it was still okay to collect the items like we'd discussed."

"Hold up." He wrote furiously. "This adds a new dimension to the case. The attack at your store happens the day *after* you started working at the mansion? The day *after* you bring Gaines's furniture to your store. By all accounts, the family is at odds after Ronald Gaines's death. You hear them arguing about…what?"

"I'm not sure. I do know Peter Gaines was angry I was even in the house. And Stella just seemed sad."

"Okay." His gaze lifted. "For now, Jasper doesn't want you or Ms. Barkley alone. TCPD stationed an officer by Shonda's room until the case is solved. As for after today—"

"I have a big job I need to finish at the Gaines mansion."

"I understand. But what you just shared complicates the case. I can't yet rule out Peter or Stella Gaines having something to do with the attack this morning." He drummed his pen on his knee. "Who contacted you about selling these items?"

"Aidan Donaldson, a couple of days after Ronald Gaines died."

"Mr. Donaldson asked you to do it?"

"Yes. It makes sense. I'm the closest antique dealer to the Gaines mansion."

"Huh. The plot thickens." Lucas tapped the recording app then set his cell on the edge of her empty hospital bed. "We'll call them in for interviews. Tomorrow or ASAP."

She let the blanket drop until it pooled over her middle. "Will I be allowed to continue gathering items from the mansion?"

He lifted his glasses off and scrubbed a hand down his face before replacing them. "I'm sorry, Brielle. But at this point, that's doubtful."

"I still have work to do. At least two more loads. Aidan had asked me to go through a few of Mr. Gaines's collections in the basement." Two days ago, she'd been ecstatic about the possibility, but now she had to admit the thought of going to that mansion by herself sent a shiver through her that had nothing to do with the cold temperatures in the hospital room.

"Not alone, you're not."

"I don't want to be foolish. Really. But I have a mortgage. Bills to pay. Clients to call back. Summer is my busiest time. And Jasper has his hands full. The baby will be here soon. They have birthing classes to take and baby prep for the cabin. My mom is finishing the farm scene mural in the baby's room. Noah and Lucy are planning their wedding."

"Which is why you'll be hanging out with me the next couple of days."

She drew back. "What do you mean?"

"Until this case is solved and the man responsible for the attack is off the streets, consider me your bodyguard."

"Don't you think that's a little extreme?"

Lucas strode over to stand by the window. From her point of view, she could see the handsome lines of his face and jaw and the veins threading his forearm muscles. He stared out into the twilight shrouding Tunnel Creek in pinks and yellows for several moments before turning to face her.

"I wasn't going to say this, but I guess it's needed." He paused, letting their gazes connect before speaking. "I believe you interrupted the man when he was about to kill Shonda. And then we interrupted him about to kill you."

Each of his steel-edged words sank deep into her bones, until Brielle's throat closed on her next breath.

"Whatever the man was after, he was willing to kill for it."

THREE

Brielle trailed Lucas through the hospital parking lot. Humid air washed over her, thawing her out after being trapped in the iceberg of a hospital room for most of the day. He walked slightly ahead of her, scanning the area, then checking to make sure she was close.

She shook her head, feeling a little like a movie star with a security detail. Had Stella Gaines experienced this with the paparazzi? Stella was once a popular actress, starring in a much-loved TV show that ran for a few seasons. Not that Brielle watched television very often, or that show in particular. She had her store to manage, plus frequent buying trips. Most nights, she returned home and crashed on her bed with a book, then fell asleep. Meals were often drive-thru, a bland microwave meal, or a much-tastier casserole dropped off by Mom.

Now, with Lucas keeping watch and her attacker on the loose, she suddenly felt like a bird stuck in a cage.

Her shoulders stiffened. Jasper and Noah had dealt with the gun traffickers in Whisper Mountain Tunnel in the not-so-distant past, but her daily life had never been touched by anything like this—so brutal and personal. She shuddered and hurried closer to Lucas.

They approached her truck, and he used her key fob to unlock the passenger-side door, then opened it for her.

"I'd like to drive in case anything occurs on the way to your house."

"Sure." Brielle climbed in, then Lucas jogged around the Tundra's bed and jumped in the driver's side, tossing his black bag onto the back bucket seats. She felt too frail to drive right now anyway—emotionally and physically.

She told him the address and pointed which way to go, and they started toward her house. "I don't think I've said thank you yet."

"Not a problem. It's my job."

"It is, but this is going above and beyond."

"I'm glad I can help your family out. And you." He hesitated. "Jasper has a lot going on right now."

She folded her seatbelt between her fingers as they headed out onto Main Street. "He does. Noah, too."

"How's your mom doing?"

"She's teaching her art classes and getting excited about the baby." Brielle was, as well. So why did thinking about her mom make her chest ache? There were moments that it felt like a splinter lodged in between her and Mom's relationship, stuck there after her dad's death in Cameroon, and Brielle had no idea if she or her mom could pull it out. It had been there so long, she'd kind of numbed herself to the pain.

"Ah, yes. Grandparents and grandbabies go together like ice cream and chocolate syrup."

She smiled. "Pretty much."

"My parents get on me about that. 'When will you get married and give us a grandchild, Lucas?'" he parroted in a higher-pitched voice. "'You're not getting any younger.' It's like I'm on trial when I come home."

She giggled. "No one's caught your eye in Myrtle Beach, huh?" She regretted the personal question as soon as it left her mouth.

"Not really. I'm busy with work, and..." Anguish seized his features, then it was gone. "Oh, I forgot to ask you something."

Brielle noted Lucas's change of subject with a soft frown. "What is it?"

"Did Shonda go with you to the Gaines mansion yesterday?"

"No, it was just me and Troy, my part-time helper."

"Where is Troy today?"

"He works at the high school as a janitor during the day and helps me in the afternoons a couple of times per week and some weekends. I would guess he's at home now since it's nighttime."

"Any reason for me to question him?"

Troy? She almost guffawed. "I don't think so. He's a single dad in his forties, lives with his teenaged son and his mom. His wife left when their son was a toddler. His mom had a stroke last year, and Troy takes care of both her and his son. He's basically a saint."

"Saints have secrets, too." His fingers tightened on the steering wheel as he slowed at a red light, his gaze faraway.

Was he thinking of Leah?

"By the way," he asked, "did Shonda always have her phone on her?"

Whatever troublesome memories had bothered him moments ago were gone now.

"Every time she was at work, yes. She might've forgotten it once or twice since she started working with me."

The light changed to green, and he glanced her way before accelerating. "When did you plan to go out to the Gaines mansion next?" His eyes darted between the road ahead and the rearview mirror, and a shiver chased down her arms.

"As soon as I can. Mr. Donaldson seemed like he wanted

the job done quickly. Apparently, he's the estate manager as well as the executor of Mr. Gaines's will. Sounds like he plans to sell the mansion."

"I'll confirm that. It's a bit unusual that Ronald Gaines asked a non-relative to be executor, instead of his own son or daughter."

"I thought so too. Maybe they've never gotten along, and Mr. Gaines thought Mr. Donaldson would keep things civil." She pointed. "Left up here."

"Possibly." Lucas flipped on his turn signal. "Mr. Donaldson sounds like he's in a hurry to get rid of some very expensive items. I wonder what *his* relationship is like with Peter and Stella."

"That I don't know. I never saw the three of them together."

"I'll find out when we interview them."

A few moments later they reached her neighborhood. The solitude of her little wooded road and sparse neighbors never bothered her before, but now all she noticed was the shadowed forest surrounding her home and its distance from town. Lucas pulled into her driveway. Her unlit front windows stared back at them like two dark, wide-open eyes, while the loft dormer window shone a pale yellow light out onto the driveway.

"Did you leave that light on?"

"Yes. It's on a timer. Comes on at eight p.m. Sometimes..."

"Sometimes you don't get home until after dark. I get it." He pointed to where her driveway met the side of the house. "No garage?"

"Nope. I figured I'd just fill it with stuff from my store." She started to push open the door. "By the way, when do I get my purse back?"

"I hope by end of day tomorrow. Hold up." Lucas exited

the truck, his eyes skimming the house and yard for several moments before he came around and ushered her out of the vehicle.

The wind hummed past, rustling the white flowers of her Carolina Silverbell and raising goose bumps on her arms.

"I'd like to go inside and check the place out first."

He pulled his black bag from the back, and she turned to take in her silent home. Night hid the porch swing and a rocking chair in its shadows, and her lawn was badly in need of a mow after all the rain they'd had lately. Even the flower beds were overgrown.

Lucas startled her as he placed a warm hand on her elbow. "Stay close."

"You're right next to me." Brielle blushed, remembering her teenage crush.

She shook it off as they headed up her walkway. Lucas peered back across the street at her only close neighbor, whose house was mostly hidden by an army of Spartan junipers. At the porch, she climbed to the second step, then stopped. One of the two large blue pots bookending the middle step was gone.

She squinted down at the side of the steps in front of her porch. The ceramic pot had fallen beside the steps, and it lay on its side, a glaring crack bisecting the middle.

"And now my morning glories bit the dust."

"What's that?" Lucas asked, instantly alert.

"One of my pots fell over. Must've been a squirrel. Or maybe a deer. They come in from the woods to munch on the flowers." She gave a soft snort. "It would be nice if they could at least eat all the grass too while they're at it."

"We'll take care of that tomorrow."

Her shoulders wilted like her poor flowers. She was so ready for this day to be over. Brielle's next step was weary and slow, and brought her shin lightly against a thin, nearly invisible piece of string stretched across the porch landing. What was that?

An audible click broke the sudden, eerie silence.

"Lucas, what—"

"Watch out!" He turned and lunged at her sideways like a linebacker making a tackle. An enormous burst of heat accompanied by an ear-splitting *boom* sent them flying off the porch as one unit. Backward. His iron embrace wrapped around her when they landed hard in the yard. Pain shot down her tailbone, and their momentum sent them tumbling through the grass.

Her breath came in short, sharp bursts when they stopped rolling. She gasped, desperate for more air, gaping at the black canvas of night dotted with yellow stars. Heat curled around her neck and face, and the fine hair on her arms felt singed. What just happened?

Had the string she felt moments ago set off a bomb?

She pulled in deep gulps of air, then struggled to sit upright. The knife wound on her side stung, and ringing filled her ears. Cool, damp potting soil and fragments of flowers covered her legs.

"Are you okay?" Lucas sounded winded like her and panicked, and one of his arms still enfolded her. "Brielle?"

A small, bright burst of orange-red flames swallowed her porch steps and railing. The sound of cracking wood brought another gasp. She swiped away a tiny, sharp-edged rock stuck to her neck, then choked down a sob.

"I'm alright." A prickle of pain, originating in her hand, traveled up her forearm. "I think."

"Be careful. There are pieces of those pots everywhere." Lucas picked off a large chunk from his jeans as he jumped up. "I need to put the fire out. Is that a hose over there?"

All she could do was nod as Lucas rushed across the yard and cranked on her hose. He hit the nozzle and sprayed the flames lapping at her porch railing and steps, then he tapped his cell and called Dispatch. She huddled on the ground in the yard, jamming a fist to her mouth and making herself as small as possible.

Someone had just blown up her front porch and her flowerpots…and she was pretty sure they'd meant for her to be standing there when it happened.

Lucas finished speaking with the paramedic, then paced toward the crime scene. He'd grabbed a pair of the remaining unused gloves from the stash Jasper had lent him at Brielle's store, along with his notepad. He needed to set boundaries around the area so the other officers didn't accidentally damage any evidence. Then he'd do a full walk-through and take pictures.

He released a hard breath. Brielle was unharmed. That was the most important thing. She had the wind knocked out of her from the impact and from shock, same as him, but appeared unhurt other than a couple of nicks from the broken pottery. Thank the Lord for that.

Lucas used yellow tape and cones to mark off the blast radius and protect what he believed to be the point of origin—the place where the bomb was planted. From what he could tell on initial search, it appeared the explosive device had been wrapped in duct tape and hidden underneath the porch swing, which sat behind a bush. In the darkness the swing was nearly impossible to see, let alone the bomb beneath it.

He finished preserving the scene, then started off around the side of the house. After unlocking the side door, he flicked on the main lights. Her house was about what he'd expect. A sturdy blue bookcase stacked with books and knickknacks served as a room divider between the living and dining room, and her galley kitchen housed black-and-white diner-type décor and a high, round table with two chairs. Artwork and old-style posters covered most of the wall space, and the scent of oranges and cinnamon helped clear out the acrid smell of smoke on his clothes from the explosion.

Along the hallway leading to the downstairs bedroom, more bookshelves lined the walls. Sometime he'd have to take a long look at her personal library.

Lucas inspected the rest of the rooms, eyed the closets and checked the bathroom.

He finished the inside—which looked completely untouched—then exited the side door, his flashlight halfway up to see what was happening with the paramedics. Brielle was still sitting on the stretcher, speaking animatedly to an EMT.

Jasper was on his way, and Chief McCoy had been notified. Lucas pressed his palm to his side and grimaced. A shard of the ceramic pot had pierced his shirt when they'd landed, leaving an angry red scratch, but he'd deal with that later. He was also grateful that the fire incited from the bomb hadn't spread more, thanks to the garden hose. While he'd hated to mess up the evidence, he also needed to stop the fire.

Time for preliminary pictures. Lucas slowly circled the warped front porch, snapping pictures with his cell. This would be easier and clearer in daylight. He gently traced the ground, looking for any pieces of the explosive device around the base of the steps.

Most of the wood was marked with black smoke, some sections were buckled; the steps and much of the front porch unpassable. The front door appeared slightly warped, the gold knob drooping and the crescent-shaped window on the upper portion broken from a projectile caused by the powerful explosion. Whoever created the homemade bomb likely hadn't gone for combustion power as much as volatile explosiveness. He used the tweezers from his back pocket to pick up a few sharp, thin shreds of metal and plastic laying on the porch.

Lucas ground his jaw as he slipped the remnants into evidence bags. Why was Brielle a target? His thoughts returned to what she shared earlier. The heated conversation she'd overheard at the Gaines mansion. Had she omitted a detail or forgotten something in the dialogue between sister and brother that made her a threat to one of the family members?

Which then begged the question responsible for Lucas's presence in town this week. Could one of Ronald Gaines's children have caused his death? Lucas was here to figure that out. But the more he learned from Brielle, the more he realized he couldn't dismiss the estate manager, Aidan Donaldson, and his possible role.

Lucas snapped another picture. He had to entertain all angles, especially since he'd seen his fair share of family feuds and bitter sibling rivalries in his line of work.

He adjusted his glasses and treaded gingerly around the edge of the blast radius. Given the circumstances, she couldn't stay at her house. His parents' gated condo community came to mind. What would Jasper think of that, for the short term?

A damp patch of dirt between the side of the house and the front walkway caught his eye. He crouched, careful not to disturb the spot. *There.* A single shoe tread mark. Not his. Definitely a man's athletic shoe of some sort. Size ten, maybe ten-and-a-half. Lucas took pictures, then marked the spot with two yellow flags.

Finally, he made his way down the driveway to Brielle.

"I'm fine. I'm just scratched up a little, and you already

took care of those." She pleaded with the paramedic. "Can I get up?"

"Not yet, ma'am." The young male paramedic glanced at Lucas nervously then back at Brielle. "I think it's best if you sit tight until…"

Her gaze narrowed, then she sighed. "Did my brother tell you to make me wait here?"

The paramedic—whose name tag said Mark—wore a bashful expression as he dipped one shoulder. "He'll be here soon."

"Lucas, help. The knife wound is rebandaged. You can see I'm okay. Don't I look okay?"

"You look fine, but that's not the issue. The issue is someone detonated an explosive device on your front porch with the intent to harm you. Jasper is just being cautious." A siren's peal carried through the woods. "There he is now."

She motioned with her chin toward her house. "Did you find anything?"

"A tread mark from a sneaker. Wires and metal pieces from the remnants of the bomb. If we recover prints, we'll see if they match the prints from your store. The inside of your house and all the windows are closed and secure. It appears whoever did this didn't break in or cause any internal damage."

Jasper's squad car kicked up gravel from the road as his car screeched to a halt on the edge of her yard. He quit the siren and jumped out, Dash leashed at his side.

"Is she okay? Brielle? Tell me what happened."

"I am okay, and I'd like to stand up."

Jasper inspected his sister, then turned to glare at the house as though it had caused the explosion on purpose.

Lucas and Brielle took turns explaining what had transpired. Then Lucas shared what he'd noticed at the crime scene moments ago.

“Sit tight,” Jasper told Brielle, then pulled Lucas with him. They walked several feet away as another officer arrived.

“I have a favor to ask.”

Lucas cocked his head. “Anything.”

“We’re stretched tight with hours at the station. We’re rotating watching Shonda, too. Most of our officers are already putting in overtime. And my cabin is kind of in baby mode. Kinsley is ‘nesting.’” He made air quotes. “I’m trying to figure out how to protect my sister and not stress out my pregnant wife, you know?”

“I understand. I’ve already considered that. Would it be alright if Brielle stays with me at my parents’ condo until we nail this guy? It’s gated, they have a guest bedroom and an alarm system on their doors and windows.”

Jasper closed his eyes briefly as relief spilled over his face. “I sure appreciate it. Your parents won’t mind a guest while they’re gone?”

“Not at all. They love your family. She can stay in their room and I’ll sleep in the guest bedroom.” His mind fast-forwarded to her case, and he dropped his voice to a hushed whisper. “I’ve been considering all the angles of these two attacks. There’s a distinct possibility Shonda and Brielle’s attacker may be connected to the Gaines family.”

“How so?”

“This started right after Brielle got the first load of furniture from the mansion yesterday. And listen to this.” He shared the conversation she’d interrupted between Peter and Stella.

“Huh. Sibling arguments. That doesn’t incriminate them, though.”

“True. But Brielle distinctly remembers Stella saying, ‘you’re the one who did this,’ to Peter Gaines.”

“I see where you’re coming from. Coincidence, or did

one of them have it out for their father and they think Brielle overheard too much?" Jasper mused.

The day's shocking turn of events flashed through Lucas's mind. "We also can't ignore this Backyard Bandit situation and a possible tie-in." He reached back, rubbing his neck. "While I don't want to add stress to the Gaines family's recent loss, we need to get to the bottom of this."

"Absolutely. I'll send a message to the Chief and get interviews lined up ASAP with the family."

"Aidan Donaldson, too. Brielle says he's the estate manager and the executor of Ronald Gaines's will."

"Gotcha. Family secrets, huh?" Jasper shifted his stance, and Dash whined and pressed his muzzle to his handler's knee. "No wonder SLED wanted his death investigated. They might've lived near Tunnel Creek, but I rarely saw them. Gaines didn't come into town much. And his kids came and went, maybe twice a year? I don't know much about his son. His daughter is an actress. She was on a popular sci-fi series a few years ago."

Lucas had never seen the show. If he watched TV, it was CSI or history shows. He had read in the report that nine-one-one was called after a family member discovered Ronald Gaines. "Any idea who actually found him?" Lucas asked.

"That I don't know. But you saw that they found him in the basement of his mansion, near the back doors, *not* in his bedroom? Which is why this whole town is convinced the Backyard Bandit had something to do with it. And why you were called in."

"I'll ask the ME for the autopsy report. It would give us a starting point with his death and if there's a possibility of any foul play." Lucas turned his head side to side, stretching his neck, as weariness crept up on him. "Which could then tie into Brielle's situation."

They turned to find her striding over.

"So, where do I go now?" She blinked forlornly at her battered porch and dark home.

"Lucas's parents' condo will work until this criminal is locked up," Jasper said.

"Lucas?" Brielle's intent gaze measured his reaction. "Is that okay?"

"Of course." He peered back at her damaged house. "You'll be safe at my parents' place."

You'll be safe...

Even as he said it, the naive simplicity of the words was eclipsed by the inherent danger of the situation. *Was* she safe? Someone—possibly a person in the Gaines family—seemed to have it out for Brielle. Now he just had to keep her safe—and find out why.

FOUR

Brielle awoke the next morning to the unmistakable scent of French toast and maple syrup. She sat up in Lucas's parents' king-size bed and rubbed the sleep from her eyes. For one glorious, peaceful moment, everything felt normal.

Then yesterday's events unfolded in her groggy brain, and the rattled, edgy feeling from last night returned like a gust of wind, blasting away the normalcy.

Shonda. Their attacker at the store. The explosion at her house.

She couldn't shake the sense that she'd never feel safe in her home or store again.

Footsteps announced Lucas in the hallway outside the bedroom.

He knocked lightly. "You up? French toast is ready."

"I'm up." Sort of. She climbed out of bed and wrapped his mom's pink knee-length robe around the T-shirt and paint-flecked plaid boxer shorts she'd slept in. Jasper had gone in her house last night and retrieved clothes for her stay at the condo. She looked down, her brows arching. *Random* was the best way to describe what her brother had chosen for her to wear.

"Be right there."

She drew her hair into a ponytail, splashed her face with cold water in the bathroom, then checked her reflection in the mirror, and finally padded into the hallway. She was exhausted and looked it. No way around that. Sleep hadn't hit until almost two a.m., and then it had been in fits. Had Lucas slept any better?

The cream-colored tile sent cold shivers up her legs as she walked down the hall. She stroked a beautiful driftwood console table topped with scripture art and a blue and brown stack of hardback books. *Books*. That reminded her. She forgot to ask Lucas which book he'd been about to give her yesterday morning. The question had nagged her last night as she'd been attempting to fall asleep. She continued down the hall, which spilled into the kitchen.

While the two-bedroom condo was modest in size, the kitchen was not. Lucas's chef mother must've chosen the floor plan for its expansive cooking and eating area. The walls were painted in bold shades of red and gold, with dark gray stainless-steel appliances. Endless counter space stretched within the large, high-ceilinged room, and a rectangular island with a full hanging pot rack accented the middle.

Lucas sat at the round, black metal table in an eating nook below a window, staring at his phone. A Bible lay open on the table, and the hanging light glared off his glasses. When he looked up, his serious expression softened. "Morning, sleepyhead."

She glanced at the microwave. Eight-forty-seven? "I never sleep in this late."

"You get a pass after what happened yesterday. How are you feeling?"

"Tired. Sore." She tucked one of the robe ties between her fingers.

"Sleep much?"

"Not really. You?" She peered at the Bible, but couldn't tell what book he was reading.

"A few hours. It'll do." Lucas kicked back in the chair and stretched his arms. She looked away from the sight of sinewy, flexing muscles beneath his white T-shirt. When her gaze returned, he motioned to the chair across from his. "You can sit. Breakfast is served."

"You don't have to ask me twice." She sank into the chair. "I wanted to ask, what book were you going to give me yesterday?"

He closed one eye and squinted. "It's a surprise. Your birthday is the twenty-fifth, right?"

"Yes, but that's like an eternity from now." She'd never been very patient.

"Ha, maybe just a couple weeks? Besides, even if I wanted to give it to you, it's in your brother's squad car. I left it there yesterday after the… When we went to your store. I'll get it later." He stood and treaded over to the black stovetop, lifted a large plate, then returned to the table. "Hungry?"

"Starving." She'd have to wait about the book. Too bad. She ogled the impressive pile of French toast he set down. "Did you make that?"

"I did." He sat. "Mind if I bless the food first?"

"Sure."

Lucas bowed his head, reaching out his hand to hers. "Thank You, God, for this food and for safety as we slept. Please grant me, Jasper, and the other officers wisdom for solving this case. And please protect Brielle and help Shonda heal. Amen."

His hands weren't as large as Jasper's or Noah's, but their strength and warmth soaked into the cool skin on her palms and fingers. She murmured *amen*, then he released her hand to offer her breakfast. She lifted a fork and stabbed two impossibly crispy yet soft pieces of French toast. After drowning them in syrup, she dug in.

Three bites later she swallowed and stared at him. "You really made this? Like, from scratch?"

He chuckled. "It's not that hard to ruin."

"I'm pretty sure mine wouldn't taste like this."

"I'm glad you like it. Despite my mom's best efforts, I can only make about four things well, and this is one of them." He cut a piece of toast, dunked it in syrup, then took a bite.

"I could eat this every day of my life." She tried not to moan or drool as she chewed, or cry when she realized it was almost gone. "What else do you make this well? I'm going to put in orders when you visit again."

"My stuffed shells aren't too bad. Lasagna is another favorite. And there's a lemon chicken piccata that my father says is better than mom's."

His bold, fleeting grin made her heart flip-flop.

Long-buried snippets of high school conversations resurfaced. "Your mom finally sold her Italian restaurant in town, right?"

"Yes. Two years ago." He downed his orange juice. "She's still trying to teach me how to make beef braciole, but I don't have the patience or the desire to spend hours in the kitchen."

"She should be very proud of your breakfast résumé. This is delicious." She popped the last bite into her mouth, savoring it, then sipped her orange juice. "Any news from Jasper? How's Shonda doing?"

"Still in ICU." He closed his Bible with a sigh. "No changes."

The mouthwatering food turned to stone in her stomach. She set the fork down. "You said you found pieces of the bomb last night. What happens next with that?"

"The evidence from the attack at your store and your house has been sent to a forensics lab in Greenville. It's the closest lab to Tunnel Creek. Conclusive results will take a couple of days at least." Lucas pushed back from the table and rose, then set his empty plate in the large sink and offered to take hers. She handed it over.

"Today we need to get your official statements." He hesitated. "From both situations yesterday. While you're doing that, I'll set up times to interview Peter and Stella Gaines, along with Aidan Donaldson."

"I gave my statement for what happened at my store already."

"Chief McCoy wants official recorded statements today." He set her plate in the sink with a soft clatter. "Sorry."

She stood slowly, the weight of a thousand questions on her shoulders. "Okay. But afterward I'd like to head to my store."

"It's still an active crime scene. You'll have to keep your store closed for at least the remainder of the week."

All the air deflated from her lungs. What was she going to do? "Can I secure the cash from the cash register at least? Make sure the back is locked up and no furniture is damaged?"

"I'll check with Jasper and see if it's alright. But I think we can do that."

Thirty minutes later they stepped into the condo's single-car garage. Inside, an apple-red Camaro was parked next to a neatly organized line of tools, a long silver workbench, and shelves stacked with storage bins.

"This is yours?" She eyed the flashy vehicle as she climbed in. It was so unlike what she'd expect Lucas to drive. "We can take my truck if you'd rather."

"No, I want your truck to stay here. We'll leave that in the driveway for now. And this show pony is a rental. Pretty tacky, right? I didn't want to put more miles on my

Explorer. Warranty is almost up," he finished by way of explanation.

"That makes sense. How far is it from Myrtle Beach?"

"It's around five hours, give or take with traffic. Just under three hundred miles." Lucas folded inside the Camaro and started it. Talk radio filled the background. He put the sports car in Reverse, then slowly backed out.

No wonder they didn't see him often. "Do your parents want you closer?"

"Sure, my mom makes comments about it. But they're mostly content that I'm in the same state at least and I'm doing well. Mom is glad I'm on the CSI team and not on patrol anymore. They're my parents. They just want me safe and happy."

"And *are* you happy?" She teased, then stumbled over her next breath. *Leah.* She of all people should know that you never really got over a loved one's death. Dad. The grief just sat on the back burner, waiting for opportunities to light up and scald you. "I'm sorry, I shouldn't have asked that."

"It's alright. You don't have to tiptoe around Leah's death. Time has helped, a little." He cleared his throat as he clicked the garage door opener clipped on the sun visor to close it.

Brielle noticed he didn't actually answer her question about being happy or not. As he drove toward the tall, wrought iron community gates, she turned the lighthearted yet telling question on herself. Was *she* happy? Not right now, that was for sure. Not with Shonda in the hospital and questions exploding like the bomb on her front porch about who this Theodore person coming after her and Shonda was.

Lucas pressed the radio knob so the background noise cut off. "So, police station first. Also, I should have your cell and wallet cleared to give back to you today. Then we'll head to your store and retrieve the money. I may take another look around."

"Thank you for this." She clutched the medium-sized tan purse he'd given her inside. "I hope your mom doesn't mind me borrowing it."

"She has a dozen purses sitting around. She won't mind at all."

While she didn't have her wallet, she did bring the burner phone Jasper gave her yesterday at the hospital, a water bottle, and tissues. Lucas remained quiet as they drove out of his parents' neighborhood. It was strange, being taken care of like this. Being chauffeured around, told what she could and couldn't do. She'd always driven herself. Directed her own schedule. Launched into her day by herself. The entire morning had been a revelation of new situations, and she found while she enjoyed Lucas's company, she wasn't a fan of feeling helpless, her life out of her control.

She wasn't a fan of being attacked either.

When they hit a red light near town, he checked his phone. "Huh. Jasper reached out to the estate manager, Aidan Donaldson. Mr. Donaldson says he's in New Jersey."

"But I just saw him the other day." Mr. Donaldson had been busy at the desk in the plush office and apartment he lived in part-time above the garage at the Gaines mansion, but he had reassured her she could take the items he'd designated from the master bedroom. "Doesn't that seem strange for him to leave so soon after Mr. Gaines died?"

"It's a bit questionable, yes." Lucas adjusted the driver's-side mirror with a frown. "This family is certainly complicated."

Brielle gazed at her surroundings and pondered her complicated relationship with her mom and family. "Aren't they all?"

He sent her a questioning look. "I'm beginning to think

there are secrets in that big house this family would rather not get out. Speaking of secrets, I contacted Troy. He was irritated when I asked his whereabouts yesterday. He's meeting me at the station in an hour."

"I might be irritated if a police officer called and questioned me, too. Doesn't mean he's guilty."

"You jump very quickly to his defense."

"Troy has been a good friend and coworker these last couple of years. He's reliable and helpful. I just think that will be a dead end." She grimaced at her poor word choice. "What does your gut say about the Gaineses' situation?"

"My gut says I ate too much French toast." Lucas peered in the rearview mirror, his brow furrowed.

"What's wrong?" She peeked behind them.

"Just keeping an eye on traffic."

Brielle nibbled on her thumbnail. They had a couple of miles until they entered Tunnel Creek, and the vivid green foliage reaching out from the woods reminded her of Noah and his job as a forest ranger.

"Did you hear Noah is engaged?" she asked.

"Yes, Jasper mentioned that. Who is she?"

"Her name is Lucy Taylor. She went to Tunnel Creek High, but only one year I think, so you wouldn't know her. We were friends."

"You were friends with everyone."

"Ha. Not true. Lexie Dunlap hated me."

"I don't think it's possible for anyone to hate you."

His sincere words soaked into the dry recesses of her heart. "Lexie liked Noah, but I wouldn't pressure him to ask her out. She believed I had some kind of power to make him like her." She wrinkled her nose. "They're my brothers, you know? It's weird. I'm not setting them up on dates."

"Sounds like there won't be a need for that anymore."

"No, there won't." She caught her bottom lip between her

teeth. "I'm really glad they're both happy." There was that word again. *Happy.* What was this twinge that made her throat tighten and her eyes smart at the thought of her brothers married and starting families? Their mom was thrilled about it all. Especially with a grandbaby about to arrive. Her mom and Kinsley had grown close over the last year.

So close, sometimes Brielle experienced pangs of jealousy. No, more like envy. She swallowed a sigh. Mom and she—well, their relationship *was* complicated. All because of what happened in Cameroon.

Dad. The last day they all saw him at their house while her parents served as missionaries in Africa. The conversation Brielle overheard between her parents, which was just as upsetting as the one she'd overheard at the Gaines mansion.

Because what she'd heard—her dad asking her mom to stay with Brielle—meant Brielle was at least partly responsible for their dad's death. Dad had gotten lost in the forest, and he wouldn't have if he and Mom had been together. Brielle was sure of it.

She sagged in the seat like a deflated airbag.

That was part of why her life revolved around work. Her store and the customers kept her going. Searching. Seeking more. Finding a treasure someone else might love fulfilled her. She couldn't deny that it was evolving into an addiction of sorts, one that Shonda had called her out on a couple months ago, when her mom had an engagement party for Noah and Lucy, but Brielle had been out of town on a buying trip and couldn't make it.

Later, Noah told her it was fine that she hadn't made it, but her normally loving brother had ended the call and hadn't replied to her follow-up text for several days. He'd been hurt.

Lucas turned abruptly down a side street. The directional

change pulled Brielle from her morose thoughts. She looked around. They were still outside Tunnel Creek, hemmed in by thick woods on both sides. Up ahead, two lonely mailboxes stood out across from each other like small wooden sentinels. The houses attached to them were tucked deep in the trees.

She frowned. "Where are we going?"

"Scenic route." He kept his gaze glued to the rearview mirror and shifted in the seat. "Looks like we're being tailed."

A chill caught hold of her skin. "Someone is following us?"

"Yes." He reached across the console and set a hand on her arm. "Do me a favor. Lean your seat way back so you're not—"

A shocking *pop* followed by the sound of the back window splintering covered his next words. Tiny bits of glass showered over her hair and the car's tight interior. Brielle screamed. Lucas thrust her down so low her forehead bumped the cup holder.

Moments later he made an abrupt right turn and accelerated, and she slammed up against the passenger-side door. The tires squealed, kicking up gravel.

"Sorry. Hang on!"

"Lucas?"

"Stay down." Another *pop* sounded, and he ducked in the seat. More flecks of glass rained down on them. Where were they? They weren't in town yet, which meant they were still in the woods somewhere.

"Did you lose them?"

His grim expression and stranglehold on the steering wheel was answer enough.

Black or dark navy truck. Male driver, slim to medium build. Dark ball cap.

Could this be Theodore Hardwick?

Jasper's observation from yesterday, at Brielle's store, lodged at the forefront of Lucas's mind. He glared at the rearview mirror as he turned down Burnt Stump Road, a pothole plagued cut-through heading into town. Once they drove over the bridge, they'd be in incorporated Tunnel Creek. And he'd have a better opportunity to draw their pursuer into a trap.

With Brielle in the car and a gun involved, playing games with this criminal was risky.

Trees hedged in the narrow gravel road. His mind shifted gears. What if another driver entered the road from the opposite direction, on the other side of the small bridge spanning the Broken Branch River they were about to cross? They'd be stuck, a rabbit between two coyotes.

He prayed that wouldn't happen. At least the driver had been so focused on keeping up with them that he hadn't fired any more shots. On the flip side, the GMC truck—a Sierra, from what he could tell—must have a V6 and horsepower to boot because it had no trouble keeping up with his base model Camaro rental.

"Keep low," he reminded Brielle. "We're going down Burnt Stump Road. Once we get across the bridge—"

"Lucas," she cried, starting to sit up. "The bridge is being repaired. It's closed!"

His mouth went slack as they sped down the final stretch of the road where the narrow bridge was indeed out. A half-dozen orange cones blocked the entrance. He didn't have time to ascertain if the bridge was still passable or just closed for cosmetic repairs.

What could they do? He had enough time and room to turn around but didn't want to risk a head-on collision with the truck. His little rental wouldn't win that fight. And getting in a shooting match with their pursuer put Brielle in harm's way. He wouldn't do that.

Which meant they had to get out and run.

"I'm going to slam the car into Park right by the woods, then we exit and take off northeast." He pointed. "That way." From what he remembered, there should only be about a mile between this road and the edge of town. Civilization. Reinforcement. He'd call in backup as soon as they were a safe enough distance from this guy.

Lucas set his jaw. *If* they made it into town. He'd forgotten how remote the area around Tunnel Creek was. How deep into the woods you could suddenly find yourself.

"Grab anything you need. Ready..." He steered left and hit Unlock on the door locks. The spewing *crunch* of stones and *crack* of dead branches spit out from the Camaro's tires and blasted through the interior. "Now!"

He slammed it into Park, then leapt from the vehicle, circling in front to help her out. They pushed through waist-high ferns and prickly thickets with desperate swipes, and ducked under low branches that swung back and stung his skin. Sprinting into the woods.

Lucas cleared a pair of small boulders as the shriek of screeching tires followed them. He'd guess they were fifty yards deep in the forest. Not far enough. Their pursuer had parked.

"Hurry," he urged.

"I am." She skirted the boulders, then squealed as a spiderweb strung between two trees caught on her face.

She swiped it away, and they weaved through the trees, his eyes panning ahead for any breaks in the woods or for any sign of buildings.

Something whistled past his head and hit a tree with a *ping*. He shouted at Brielle. "Keep low and zigzag," he shouted. "He's shooting."

She veered to the right, away from him, then disappeared into a thicket. He scrambled to follow her and place himself between her and the shooter. The *slam* of a car door taunted them from the roadside. Their pursuer was out of the vehicle and on foot now, too.

Lucas's breaths roared in and out as he edged around a massive stump then connected back up with Brielle. He grasped her arm and pulled her beside him. When they came upon a small creek, he urged her on.

"Keep going." He pushed her from behind.

She splashed through the water and he followed, then they dashed into the woods on the other side. Her elbow accidentally caught his rib as they crossed overtop a rotting tree blocking their path. Brielle muttered an apology as they both slowed, looking around. Sweat circled his forehead and dripped down his brow. A bird squawked from a branch overhead. A warning.

"Do you know…where we are?" he asked.

"Long's Lumber. Is up here." She pointed, trying to catch her breath. "We can cut through, and there's a road on the other side of their barn. This way."

Long's Lumber? He'd never heard of it. She took off at a fast jog, and Lucas kicked off the ground after her. The forest thinned out into a meadow, which was helpful for picking up speed but made them easier targets. Rays of sunlight flashed down on them as they passed through the grassy field at a breakneck speed.

Once they entered the tree line on the other side of the meadow, Lucas slowed and chanced a look back. Had they lost the armed man? He snatched his cell from his pocket, hit 911, then the speaker button.

The dispatcher's voice came on. "Nine-one-one, what's your emergency?"

"This is Lucas Scott," he shouted, as he slogged uphill after Brielle. The terrain rose in an incline, and their pace slowed, his lungs screaming for air. "Brielle Holt and I are being chased by an armed man. Shots fired. We're on foot in the woods. Near Burnt Stump Road. Approaching Long's Lumber now."

Brielle stopped near the top, bracing her arm on a tree and staring downhill.

A valley spread out, dotted with a few large barns, multiple lean-tos packed with wood, and massive stacks of finished and unfinished lumber. A big rig fitted with lifting equipment was parked on the far side, at the end of a winding driveway.

"Are you in a safe location?" the woman asked.

"Trying. To get there." He surveyed the barns below, his eyes stinging from sweat. "Plan is to go into one of the barns at Long's Lumber."

"I'm sending an officer out there now."

"Might want to send two." He disconnected the call.

The shriek of a sawblade carried on the wind like a warning. The fact that they were stuck between a dangerous armed man and a sawmill yard loaded with sharp machinery and piles of heavy, stacked logs made his muscles constrict.

"Where…do we go…now?" Brielle panted.

The *zing*, *whomp* of a bullet hitting a nearby tree sent Lucas down, one arm flung around Brielle to bring her with him. They crashed to the ground. Pine needles stuck to his cheeks and neck, and pebbles dug into his knees. He pushed his glasses back up on his nose.

"He's catching up." Lucas spit out a clump of dirt. "We have to run. Go to that large gray barn. It looks close enough and secure. Hide behind the lumber if he starts shooting again."

"Stay close to me, please." Her lovely eyes were rounded, and he hated the fear he saw in them.

"I'll be right beside you." He held her gaze. "Remember, we're not alone. God is with us."

She gave a wobbly nod, then they jumped to their feet and ran down the hill toward the lumberyard.

God, please protect us. Keep Brielle safe.

"Go! The first pile of logs." He motioned as they sprinted toward the gray barn. A twenty-foot-high pile of logs lay in the yard halfway there, and she dove right as he went left. His chest tightened from the exertion and from being separated from her. When she appeared on the other side, he gulped in a wobbly breath.

They sprinted side by side to the barn. Lucas lunged at the wide, heavy double doors, yanking one open. He pulled her inside, then drew the door shut. The world suddenly stopped moving and he clenched his eyes shut for a moment as his raging heartbeat slowed.

Brielle gasped beside him.

"What is it?" Lucas pivoted to find a massive hanging rack loaded with sharp, angry-looking equipment. Silvery blades and serrated saws hung over their heads on racks, while other pieces were set on shelving on and along the barn walls.

Brielle bent over, hands on her knees, chest heaving. "I think we chose. The wrong building."

Lucas tugged out his Glock and flicked off the safety. It would have to do. The gunshots came from the woods behind them, which meant the shooter had tracked them here and was likely at the wood's edge by now. Giving them only a minute or less to prepare.

"Do me a favor," he said, clearing sweat from his forehead. "Go hide, back there." He pointed to an open stall on the barn's side. "Watch yourself. Everything in here is sharp."

"No kidding." She darted over to the stall and disappeared behind it, then he slunk toward the window beside the doors.

"I can't imagine this guy will try something at an open location like this, where anyone can see his face. But we have to get ready in case he makes it to this door."

"Did you get a look at him?"

"Not in great detail. He was wearing a ball cap, sunglasses. Has brown hair, I think."

"So, he's not wearing a mask like when he was in my store?"

"No." Lucas peered through the hazy glass panels of the rectangular window. The barn was older, and faint cracks in the wood let in sunlight. A musty scent—wood, hay, and dirt—permeated the building.

The man must've waited outside his parents' condo community for them. Had he followed them there last night, after they left Brielle's house? Lucas had watched for a tail but hadn't noticed anything out of the ordinary. Then again, it had been near midnight when they'd left her house, and he'd been exhausted.

His cell buzzed. Talk about poor timing. He ignored it, but after two cycles of buzzing eight times then stopping plus no sign of their pursuer, Lucas tugged the phone from his pocket and opened the screen.

Jasper.

Lucas hit the speaker button. "We're at Long's Lumber. Safe inside a barn. She's unharmed. I called in backup about four minutes ago."

"We're two minutes away."

"Glad to hear it."

"Brielle's okay?"

Lucas glanced behind him. Brielle peeked out from the stall, her dark brows drawn together. "Yes. I've got her hidden."

"What happened?"

"Pursued from my parents' condo. Shots fired. Cracked the rental's back window. The truck tailed us about a half mile from their community gates. Appears to be the truck you saw yesterday. I made several turns, then took Burnt Stump Road thinking it would lead into town." He frowned. "Bad move."

"You didn't know the bridge was out."

"Yeah, well, we ended up at this place. We're hunkered down in a large gray barn. Looks like equipment storage. I'm worried about civilian casualties."

An explosion of fragmented wood and glass showered him, and a cold weight gathered in his core. Someone had shot out the window. They'd been found.

FIVE

Brielle cowered behind the wood stall as Lucas crouched below the window near the door, his eyes fierce behind his glasses and his gun aimed at the door.

He peered up at the broken window then back at her. Dust motes kicked up in the air between them from the window breaking, and glass glittered around him like sharp, oversize raindrops. Jasper would be there soon. That gave her a measure of peace. So did the determined man guarding the door. *Lucas*. Had he been struck by any of the bullets? Or the glass?

"Are you okay?" she asked.

Another gunshot rang out, this one farther away. Brielle squealed and tucked into a ball. Then a man's shout carried over, along with the sound of barking dogs. She peeped out, her gaze landing on Lucas.

Is that backup? she mouthed.

He wore a thoughtful frown but shook his head. *Wait*, he mouthed.

The sound of lumbering footsteps and jangling tags followed.

"Someone's coming." She held a wad of air in her cheeks.

"That's not the gunman." Lucas kicked the door open partway but stayed inside, his features drawn tight. "I'm

Lucas Scott with SLED. I'm an armed law enforcement agent. Identify yourself."

"What're you people doing in my barn?"

Henry Long's voice. She released the breath and stood on shaky legs. "That's Mr. Long. He owns this place."

"Sir, there was an armed gunman chasing us." Lucas informed him. "Tailed us from Hawk's Reserve, my parents' condo community."

"Not anymore." The door swung wide. Henry Long entered, his tan overalls and worn green Long's Lumber T-shirt stretched taut by his formidable middle. A pair of black-and-tan German shepherds followed, their tongues lolling and expressions alert.

"Gable. Stewart. Ease up, boys. Go say hello," he commanded the large dogs. They sniffed Lucas, then trotted over to her.

She held her palms out for the dogs to sniff, then scratched their large ears. "Hi, puppies. I'm sure glad to see you two. Mr. Long, I'm sorry this happened at your place. We didn't have anywhere else to go."

"Who on earth is after you?" Mr. Long snatched his hat off and rubbed his forehead. His thick salt-and-pepper hair stuck out in all directions, and his face was creased like old leather from the years spent outside.

"An armed suspect was pursuing us," Lucas said. "I came down Burnt Stump Road and—"

"And the bridge is out. Ah, yes." Henry shifted his considerable frame. "But why's that guy after you?"

"We have an open investigation involving Ms. Holt and her store. I'm afraid that's all I can say at this time." Lucas holstered his gun.

"We love Ms. Holt around here. I don't take kindly to someone trying to hurt her or rob her store."

"Neither do I," Lucas returned.

Henry grunted his approval. "My wife, Dot, needed some sort of fancy table for her sewing machine, and this here young lady found her one." He winked at Brielle. "She was right pleased with it. You make Dot happy, you make *me* happy."

Brielle beamed. "I'm so glad she loves the table."

Henry continued. "She was just talking about taking a drive out to your store soon, matter of fact."

"I'm sorry, but it's closed." Lucas spoke before Brielle could answer. "Police investigation."

"Hmm. I did hear about some scuffle. And that Ms. Barkley's in the hospital. Martha told Dot that at Bill's Pharmacy. Terrible shame. Are you okay?" Henry asked Brielle. "Jasper'll skin me alive if you get hurt at my place."

"I'm okay, Mr. Long. Thank you." She nodded at Lucas. "He kept me safe."

Mr. Long glanced between them, his gaze settling on Lucas. "Who'd you say you were?"

"Lucas Scott, South Carolina Law Enforcement Department. I work in crime scene investigations in Myrtle Beach."

"He used to live here," she volunteered.

"Ah, is that so." Henry cocked his head in thought. "Scott. Scott, hmm."

"I'm in town staying at my parents' place." He relayed their names, but that was it. He didn't need to reveal that he was also in town investigating Ronald Gaines's death.

"That's it. Roseanne Scott. Dot and I sure enjoyed that restaurant of hers. Was real sad when she sold it and they turned that building into one of those fancy coffee places. It's hard to find good meatballs in this town."

Lucas and Brielle shared a tiny smile, then Lucas answered. "She misses the people, but not the hours. Right now, they're in Europe." He peered through the window. "Did you happen to get a look at the shooter?"

"Can't say I did. 'Specially after I shot back." Henry gripped the large weapon in his grasp and grinned at Lucas. "Definitely a man. Wearing black, I think."

Sirens wailed their arrival, and Brielle stepped out from the stall. She addressed Mr. Long. "I'm sorry about the window."

"That's alright. It'll fix. Just glad you kids are okay."

She pressed a careful hand to her side. Thankfully the bandage over the knife wound was still stuck on. After their run and almost getting shot in the back, she didn't feel like a *kid*. The last twenty-four hours had surely aged her. Her thoughts turned a corner as she noted Lucas's taut posture. He hadn't come here to be a bodyguard. Now he was being chased through the woods and getting shot at. Guilt nipped at her like a little terrier.

Lucas motioned her over. "Let's get you out of here."

Several minutes later, after a grilling from Jasper and careful perusal of sketches on Jasper's iPad to see if they recognized the suspect, she and Lucas stood beside an unmarked police car. The second officer, Chris Anders, had arrived moments after Jasper.

"We'll get your rental towed once I get your statements." Officer Anders climbed into Jasper's squad car as Brielle and Lucas headed toward Officer Anders' police car, which they'd drive to the station.

A thought struck her mid-stride. *The purse.* "Your mom's purse. I dropped it back there. I should go get it."

"I'll come along," Lucas said.

They changed course and headed toward the large stack of lumber.

"Where are you going?" Jasper rolled his window down and called after them.

"Lucas lent me one of his mom's purses, and I dropped it back here." She trotted toward the lumber pile, then spun in a slow circle, surveying the yard. No sign of it.

Brielle frowned. She was certain she'd run this way, and the strap had gotten caught on the log sticking out right there.

Lucas trailed over. "See anything?"

"I'm almost positive I lost it here. But no, nothing." She pointed to a squashed clump of wildflowers at the base of the stacked wood. Directly in the path of the barn where they'd hidden. "I know I had it when we sprinted out of the woods. It was bumping into my side as we ran."

But the purse wasn't there.

Lucas crouched, fingering the dirt. Then he removed his cell and snapped pictures. "There are shoe treads here. Larger than yours. See how they circle this spot? Looks like our suspect grabbed it before he ran."

She tilted her face to the sky and closed her eyes. "I'm sorry, Lucas." Why couldn't anything go right?

"I don't care about the purse. Besides, this may be a good thing."

"How?" She reopened her eyes and sent him a questioning look.

"We might be able to track him." He stood, slipped his cell back in his pocket. "Jasper," he called out, then strode over to her brother's squad car. "Looks like the shooter has her purse. Can you track the burner phone you gave her?"

"On it." Jasper fiddled with something in his lap, probably his own cell.

As the two men talked, Brielle pushed the tip of her shoe into a cluster of stones, then sent them flying. They scattered a few inches apart, rearranged. A sigh built in her chest. She loved her family. Her mom, Jasper, Noah, Kinsley, and now Lucy. Especially her sweet nephew, Gabe. But for some reason, she was different from them. Separate.

She released the sigh. Maybe it was because of what happened with Dad.

Jasper and Noah didn't know their mom had stayed behind that day because of Brielle, despite the fact that her mom was better at directions and knew the area they'd lived in well. Brielle winced. She couldn't let them find out. They'd blame her for their dad's death.

Just like she already did. Like Mom probably did, too. Was that why Mom was always so hesitant around her?

Did Brielle remind Mom of that horrible day Dad died?

Her thoughts dialed backward twenty or so years. When her dad had left their little house on a hill beside the school to bring supplies to a neighboring school. A half-day trip he'd only ever taken with her mom.

But dad had gotten lost…and never returned.

And it was her fault. Just like she had a feeling Shonda's attack was.

Her vision clouded with tears. She blinked furiously, focusing her mind on something positive, like how much she loved helping clients like Dot Long. Months ago, Dot had been on the lookout for an old-style treadle Singer sewing table for her ancient sewing machine. When Brielle finally located the table, Dot had been so thrilled she'd hugged Brielle and promptly sewn her an oven mitt and an apron two sizes too large.

Lucas brushed up next to her. "Jasper is sending an officer to check the woods between here and my rental car. And check the car. We'll have it towed to a shop to check for damage." He paused, his eyes pinned to her face. "Hey, what is it?"

The shriek of spinning saws mutilating wood started up again, punctuating his gentle question.

"I'm scared, Lucas. Someone could've been killed today. You. Mr. Long. And then there's poor Shonda."

"Shonda is safe. She's improving."

Brielle shook her head. "She has an armed guard at her hospital room door, and you're glued to my side like I'm a criminal."

"You're not the criminal here." He growled softly. "And this isn't your fault."

"Lucas," Jasper called out, interrupting their exchange. "The shooter must've shut her burner phone off. We'll see if the company can track it. Right now, we're heading to the station. You two coming?"

"We're coming. I have an interview in ten minutes." Lucas returned his attention to Brielle. "I'm sorry, we need to get going. Troy will be waiting for me."

Twenty minutes later, she sat in one of the wooden chairs facing Chief McCoy's desk. She'd known the chief for several years, given Tunnel Creek's small population and Jasper's position at the police station. While his snarl was mostly for show, he was still a short-fused man who didn't suffer fools. He sat ramrod straight in his chair, short-cropped hair speckled with gray, his hands rubbing his grizzled cheeks.

Lucas was interviewing Troy in the office next door, and Jasper had left to be with Kinsley, who was experiencing strong enough contractions she'd called her doctor for advice.

She rubbed her clammy hands down her shorts. Were Kinsley and the baby okay?

"Ms. Holt, I've gone over your statement of what happened at your store. Both Mr. Gaines and Ms. Gaines have solid alibis for yesterday morning. They were on a call with the lawyer who represented their father. The lawyer's secretary confirmed it."

"But it was the other person—Theodore something—who came after me, right?"

"Correct."

A knock sounded, then Lucas appeared through a crack in the door. "Mind if I join you?"

"Come in," McCoy answered. "How'd it go with Troy Hanson?"

"Airtight alibi. He was at a doctor appointment with his son." Lucas settled in the chair next to Brielle's, facing McCoy's desk.

McCoy repeated what he'd just told Brielle about Peter and Stella Gaines.

Lucas gave a shrug. "So the Gaines siblings have alibis. That's to be expected. We know they didn't personally commit the crime. Theodore Hardwick did."

"Allegedly," McCoy interjected.

"Allegedly," Lucas repeated. "But if the prints match..." He left the sentence hanging for a long moment. "I'd still like to interview them myself, sir. All three of them. Donaldson, too."

"You don't need my permission to do that." Chief McCoy's hooded gaze sharpened on Lucas. "In addition, I spoke with Mr. Donaldson. There was a family wedding he attended in New Jersey, and he's flying back later tonight."

"Family wedding? Seems rather conveniently timed," Lucas muttered. "Especially if he—or Peter—had a hitman set up. Looks good for them if they're gone."

"I get it." McCoy tossed his pen on the desk. "We have an APB out for Theodore Hardwick. If he's in the area, we'll catch him. We're trying to cross-reference any prints from the Backyard Bandit's last break-in. It's in the next county over, unfortunately, and Chief Andrews isn't always easy to work with. Tying Mr. Hardwick to the Gaines family is essential. Even if Ms. Holt overheard incriminating evidence of foul play—and it doesn't necessarily sound like that's what she heard—why did the attacker go after Ms. Barkley, her coworker?"

"If there is a connection with the Gaines family, maybe it's because Peter Gaines thinks I heard more than I actually did?" she volunteered.

"Possibly," McCoy admitted. "The facts remain that Ms. Barkley's cell is missing. Theodore Hardwick is on the run. This case is still developing by the hour." McCoy addressed Brielle. "Because of that, I'd like you to lay low until further notice. Don't go to your store—"

"Chief McCoy, please." She threw Lucas a pleading look. "The only way for me to get any work done is at my store. Working remotely isn't an option."

"You may collect the money from the cash register and any personal items you left. But close-up shop. The community understands. Put a sign on the door until we catch this guy."

"It's not just the community. It's the timing. It's summer. Tourists drive through here to see Whisper Mountain Tunnel and go hiking. See the waterfalls. Summer is my busiest time."

"While I understand that, we're not breaking protocol so you can make a buck."

She drew back as though he'd slapped her.

"Chief McCoy," Lucas interrupted, his blue eyes flickering her way and offering a gentle warning behind his glasses. "I'm going to take Brielle to her store today and let her take care of those things."

"How long do I have to keep my doors closed?" she asked.

"That's hard to say at this point." Chief McCoy settled his beefy forearms on his desk. "Ms. Holt, I believe—and I know your brother does too—that your life is more important than selling antiques."

Her shoulders drooped at the cold-water effect his words had. While she logically understood what he was saying, she couldn't comprehend shutting her store down for days, maybe even a week.

Still, what choice did she have? "Yes, sir."

Chief McCoy dismissed them, and they made their way to a white, unmarked Charger. Lucas's rental car was impounded as two officers combed through it, then it would head over to the police mechanic for a diagnostic and to have the broken glass replaced.

Once they settled inside the vehicle, she closed her eyes and massaged her brows. "I'm sorry. I almost lost it in there."

"You did fine. McCoy's the king of curmudgeons, but he does care." He hesitated, then settled his warm palm on her arm. "We're all worried about you. We want this case solved so you can go back to your normal life."

"Thank you, Lucas." His presence and the considerate, caring way he looked after her during this difficult time lifted her spirits and reminded her why she had crushed on him all those years ago.

But nothing could touch the uncomfortable weight pressing down on her chest, knowing that they had a long way to go before this case was solved. The man who tried to kill her was still on the loose.

And until he was caught, she was in grave danger.

Lucas pulled out of the police station, his thoughts racing.

Before Jasper left to join his wife at the doctor's office, he and Lucas had briefly gone over his phone conversation with Peter Gaines. While it wasn't an official interview, Jasper had questioned Peter about his and Stella's whereabouts yesterday. Apparently, Peter had been impatient and defensive on the phone, then shut down when prodded about his relationship with Stella. Jasper believed Peter was hiding something related to Stella.

When Jasper had spoken to Stella, he said she'd started off weepy and stayed that way through the short conversation. Fragile, Jasper noted to Lucas. A little odd, but for the most part she just seemed exhausted and overcome by grief, he'd said.

And then there was Troy Hanson, Brielle's coworker, who also had an alibi. Troy clearly held Brielle in high esteem. Possibly had a crush on her. Which was understandable. Brielle was attractive, smart, caring. Troy was quite a bit older, but that didn't bother some.

He loosened his stranglehold on the wheel. Sometimes unrequited romantic crushes could turn into obsession. A sour taste spread over his tongue.

"It's too bad Troy didn't overhear what was said that night, too." He was curious how she'd respond to his observation. "He wasn't standing next to you, near the master bedroom?"

"No. He stayed in the foyer. I was checking to see if the room was clear." She glanced at him. "Why? What did Troy say?"

"He repeated what you told him later. He said he stayed near the front doors. Thinks very highly of you, and he's worried about your well-being like the rest of us."

"Troy is a great guy, and he has been a huge help at work with the bigger pieces of furniture."

Lucas tamped down an unnecessary remark about Troy's interest in her. Saying it aloud would accomplish nothing. Talking to Troy about Brielle and talking to Brielle about Troy made him unaccountably irritable, so he dropped it.

"I'm going to grab lunch up here—" He pointed to Clucker's Chicken, a local drive-through on the right.

Cheap and greasy, just the way he didn't like his food. His mom would do her own clucking if she knew he was even considering eating there. "Is that okay?"

"I don't have much of an appetite, but if you're hungry, go for it."

He pulled into the packed parking lot. School was out. That explained the influx of children and families running every which way. The drive-through was several cars deep, and people streamed through the doors for the dining area like ants on their way to a dropped fry. "You want to grab the food and head to your store, or eat here?"

"Do you mind just grabbing the food? I have utensils, napkins, and water at my store. I'd rather eat there." She leaned her head back on the headrest. "Didn't we just eat breakfast?"

"It's almost one. I worked out before you woke up. Then there was that run through the woods. Remember?"

"Unfortunately, yes."

He checked out the lot for several seconds, then steered toward the drive-through. At the last minute, a minivan weaved around him and got in line. Bringing the total number of cars waiting to at least seven or eight.

"Why don't you just go in? I'll wait out here."

He checked the doors. People were filing in and out quickly. Drive-through? Not so much. Okay. Order inside it would be.

He pulled into a parking spot beside another minivan. "I'd prefer you come in with me."

"Please, Lucas. I'm a mess."

"You're not a mess. You look fine. More than fine." He clenched his jaw as she turned toward him, her lovely hazel eyes widening.

"Please, can you lock the car doors? Aren't these bulletproof windows?"

"Doubt it. TCPD is a small force in a smaller town, and this isn't a fully loaded squad car. They don't have money for upgrades." Indecision warred. There were families sitting on the benches just outside the restaurant, and a teenage couple locking arms and lips beside them.

"Here's my cell if there's any trouble." He had her input the number in the second black burner phone they'd given her. "Call or text, then call nine-one-one if anything happens."

She nodded, then told him what she wanted. He exited the vehicle, his gaze roving the parking lot. If the shooter came after Brielle here, he would be seen by two dozen or more eyewitnesses. Surely, he wasn't that brazen.

Lucas strode inside, brushing past the metal, human-sized rooster statue in the front lobby. He inspected the store for any customers who fit his very fluid description of Theodore Hardwick. None here. And the line was only three deep. Excellent.

Five minutes later, cell in hand, he waited at the pick-up counter. Every few seconds Lucas pivoted to peer through the windowed doors. So far nothing suspicious happened.

His cell buzzed. A text from Jasper.

They found Brielle's burner phone in the woods near the bridge where you parked. Suspect must've realized we might be able to trace it. I'll have them check it for prints.

Too bad. Lucas blew out a hard breath, then typed a quick response.

Moments later his cell buzzed again. Wasn't Jasper supposed to be with his wife? Why—

Not Jasper. Brielle.

Someone just walked around the car. Looked inside. Man with a ball cap.

Lucas spun and dashed toward the doors, his hand on his weapon. "Officer on duty! Out of the way."

He burst through the restaurant door, the thick humidity outside choking him. His gaze immediately sought the unmarked police car. Brielle. She was still safely in the vehicle, but ten yards past the car a tall man with a dark ball cap loped through the gas station beside Clucker's. Lucas sprinted across the parking lot and patted the passenger window, mouthing, *Stay put.* Then he took off after the suspect.

Adrenaline burned his veins like wildfire through dry brush. "Stop! Police. Turn around and put your hands out."

The ball-cap-wearing suspect kept running. Lucas shouted at a young man at the gas pump who tried to stop the suspect and ended up getting shoved. "Police. Get inside your vehicle."

The hot concrete jarred his knees as he flew past the pumps and the car wash. On the other side of the gas station sat a brick, two-story home renovated into a hair salon. Past that, a strip mall backed up to a large stretch of woods connecting to Sumter National Forest.

"Stop! Put your hands up and turn around," he shouted again.

The suspect lunged behind a concrete pole, ignoring him, then sprinting on. Lucas's lungs screamed for air as he followed. The distance between them decreased, but the man was quickly closing in on the woods behind the strip mall. When the suspect reached the strip mall, he slowed to weave through cars and trucks parked in front of a hardware store. Then he ducked and disappeared. Lucas trailed doggedly after him, warning people to stay in their cars. Suddenly the man darted between two stores. Must be a break in the mall building. Lucas changed directions, but when he reached the end of the open, covered corridor between the stores, the suspect had disappeared into the trees.

Lucas ground his jaw. Too bad Jasper and Dash weren't here. They would've had the suspect caught and down by now, no doubt.

He scanned the ground for any items the man might have dropped. In a section of damp dirt, he noted the tread marks. Similar—or the same—as the treads from Brielle's yard last night and the lumberyard earlier today. He snapped pictures with his phone, then jogged back to Clucker's. On the way, he called in the incident, adding the description of the suspect.

Brielle scrambled out of the car. "Lucas, are you okay?"

"I'd be better if I caught the guy." The young couple beside them gaped at his sweaty, wind-blown appearance and his Glock. He holstered it, then addressed them. "Did you see the man who walked past this car? About five-ten, one-eighty, dark hair, blue ball cap?"

"I don't know." The young man shrugged. "I just saw a guy with a hat and some dope shoes."

Lucas cocked his head. "What kind of shoes?"

The kid rattled off the name of fancy sneakers. Lucas looked them up on his cell while they waited for the other officer to arrive. Available at large departments stores for a pretty penny. More like fifty thousand pennies. No wonder the treads he'd noticed at Brielle's house had stood out. So, Theodore Hardwick had expensive taste. Which meant the man either had a connection to money somewhere, or he stole them. Interesting.

Sirens sounded as another TCPD officer approached then pulled in. Matt Reed parked behind them and stepped out of the vehicle. "Ms. Holt. Agent Scott." He gripped his utility belt as he walked over. "Heard you had another run-in with the suspect?"

"I believe we did." Lucas rattled off the play-by-play of the last fifteen minutes.

Brielle stepped up next to Lucas and set her hand on his arm. The warmth of her touch deleted his next thought like a backspace button.

"Where did our food go?" she whispered.

The food. Right. He glanced across at Matt. "Do you mind getting her statement while I grab our order? Be right back."

Officer Reed nodded, then began questioning Brielle.

Lucas trotted inside, thanked the curious employees behind the counter for keeping their food safe, and returned to the parking lot. Brielle now leaned against the unmarked car, her arms twined over her middle and her wavy brown hair tossed by the wind. When her hazel eyes met his, it felt like a gut-punch.

What was *that*? This was Brielle Holt. Jasper's sister.

Exactly. Jasper's *sister.* He wiped the remaining sweat from his brow and glared up at the stormy sky, trying to ignore his strange reaction to his best friend's beautiful little sister. *Stop it, Scott.*

He almost stumbled as he stepped off the curb. All these years later, he still blamed himself for what happened to Leah. And Jasper would never agree to a man like him—a man whose selfish and irresponsible behavior led to his fiancé's death—dating his younger sister.

He straightened his spine and headed over. Once Matt finished asking her questions, Lucas and Brielle loaded into the vehicle. He gave Matt a goodbye salute. The other officer pulled away, and Lucas followed slowly, getting back on the main road before doing a U-turn and heading east to her store.

"Do you want to eat now?" he asked.

"Not really. I'll eat at my store."

"How'd it go with Matt? Were you able to describe the suspect's features at all?"

"A little bit. It happened so fast that by the time I realized it might be the guy, I had to focus on my text to you."

"Speaking of texts. Your brother texted right before you did. They found your burner phone in the woods we ran through. Near where my rental was parked."

"So, he dropped it?"

"Appears so." He glanced her way, noting her bleak expression and clenched hands, then followed the sudden urge to try to lift her spirits. "What's your favorite part about your job?"

"The joy of a good find." She paused. "I get to connect a lovingly used item with a new owner. Sometimes even handpick them. Customer treasures, Shonda calls them."

"Nice. Mr. Long seemed grateful for that skill of yours. And it reminds me of what I read this morning in my Bible."

"What was that?"

"I'm in Matthew six. 'Lay up for yourselves treasures in heaven, where neither moth nor rust doth corrupt, and where thieves do not break through nor steal: For where your treasure is, there will your heart be also.'"

She scrunched the top of the fast-food bag. "I understand they're just things, Lucas. I don't… I try not to put their importance and value above people."

"Hey, I didn't mean that. I know your work is important and meaningful to you."

She stared straight ahead, not answering. His jaw ticked. He shouldn't have brought up the Bible verse.

Lucas gnawed the inside of his cheek as he followed the road. He knew the drive to her store well because one of his high school friends, Terrence, lived out here with his mom. Last he heard, Terrence had gotten his welder's license and worked at a metal factory in Tunnel Creek. His friendship with Terrence was another thing he'd lost after Leah's death. It had been difficult staying in Tunnel Creek, where guilt was easily accessible and memories haunted every corner.

Moments later her store came into sight, a silver Lexus SUV parked in the lot.

"Who is that?" Lucas asked.

"I don't know. I don't recognize the car. A customer, maybe?"

They both stared at the SUV as Lucas pulled in.

"For now, stay in the car, please. Let me speak to them first." He could make out a male in the front seat. Smaller frame. Clean-shaven, short-cropped brown hair. The man turned to them with a tight expression when Lucas parked three spots down from him.

Brielle released a slow, pinched breath. "That's Peter Gaines."

What was he doing at Brielle's store? Lucas unbuckled and patted his side, checking his weapon. He was about to find out.

SIX

Brielle clutched the fast-food bag as Lucas strode toward the silver Lexus, his back ramrod straight. His intelligence, serious demeanor, and intimidating build gave off the message not to mess with him.

Please God, protect him.

It felt strange, praying again. Almost like speaking a foreign language she had to relearn. Would God listen to her prayers even with her faith still shaky?

Words filled her mind, unbidden but faithful. Words connected to tucked-away, childhood memories from Cameroon, when her family consisted of five people, not four. Words she memorized before Dad's death and refused to utter afterward.

"For thou art my Hope, O Lord God; Thou art my trust from my youth."

She unbuckled her seat belt, folding it between her fingers over and over as she watched Lucas and Peter's tense conversation. Finally, Lucas stepped back, and Peter rolled up his window and reversed out of the spot, his sleek SUV creating a dust cloud as he flew out of the parking lot. When he passed by, he sent a glacial glare at Brielle.

Lucas waited until he drove away then he retrieved his cell from his pocket to call someone. Chief McCoy? Jasper? She pressed a palm to her chest. What had he been doing at her store?

Lucas hung up and jogged over to open the passenger-side door. She exited on unsteady legs, the rumpled fast-food bag in her grasp, and followed him up the walkway to the front doors. She stopped short at the bright yellow tape that said "Police Line Do Not Cross" strung across the entrance.

Brielle snorted softly. "I guess this is a bad time to joke about not crossing the line?"

"Yeah. We'll have to duck underneath. What's the code?"

She told him, and he punched it in, then climbed below the tape to open the door. She handed him the food bag and followed, squatting low and clambering inside, then stood and nudged the light switch on with one elbow.

Lucas trailed her as she found a small card table half full with domino and marble sets, placing the food on it. He peered around as she hurried across the store and rounded the corner to reach the small fridge beneath the register. She pulled out two waters, then returned to the front area by the doors.

"What was that about out there?" She nodded back at the parking lot.

"Mr. Gaines is upset that you have his father's items." He opened the bag and withdrew his sandwich. "He wants them back."

"That matches up with what he said to his sister in his father's bedroom."

"Right, but at this point in the investigation, I don't think it's best for you to return everything."

A boulder settled on her chest as Lucas unwrapped then bit into his chicken sandwich. "Do you think—" she motioned at the storage room, then at herself "—that Peter Gaines believes I *stole* these items? Or that I'm going to steal them?"

"No. He knows Mr. Donaldson and his sister okayed you taking them. He just wants everything back."

She swallowed. "Shonda and I were planning to do appraisals yesterday. That and taking pictures to list the items online. I have a website where my larger items are listed."

"Right. Jasper mentioned that."

"Plus, we had more to pick up from the mansion."

Lucas looked around as he chewed and swallowed another bite. "Your store is pretty packed. Where were you going to put the rest of the items?"

"We can fit a lot in the back storage room. And I have the shed out back. It's air conditioned and fairly roomy. I was also going to rent a storage unit in town. Just for this job."

"That's an extra expense, right?"

"It is," she admitted. "But Mr. Donaldson offered enough to cover an additional storage space for several months. He just wanted the things moved…quickly." Part of why she'd jumped at this job. Sometimes it took clients—or their families—days, weeks, even a month to finally part with the item or items they'd contacted her about. Parting with loved ones' treasured possessions was painful. Final. Occasionally they changed their minds.

Lucas accepted the bottle of water she handed him, then took a long drink before continuing. "I'd prefer you not contact Mr. Donaldson at this point."

Brielle tucked her lips to her teeth. "I texted him while I was waiting at the restaurant. Just mentioned I might be heading to the mansion later today in case he wanted me to take a look at anything. Is it bad that I texted him?"

"It's alright, but from now on please let me talk to him." He finished the water and she motioned for the bottle so she could throw it in recycling.

He looked around. "So, you pay the client back once you sell the item?"

"In this case, yes. I let the client know what I'm getting for the item, plus a small markup. There's a lot of back and forth." She scratched her thumbnails together. "In the Gaineses' situation, it appears there isn't an issue with family money and relatives wanting or needing it immediately."

"I wouldn't assume that." He finished the last bite of his sandwich and wiped his mouth with a napkin. "We're still doing background checks for Mr. Donaldson, Stella, and Peter. Even Ronald Gaines. Might be skeletons—financial or otherwise—hiding in those closets."

Brielle shuddered at that mental image.

"Mr. Donaldson seems to be the engine driving this vehicle. Which is another reason I'd like to be the one communicating with him." Lucas stared past her at the mirror she'd seen her reflection in yesterday morning. She turned.

"That mirror is the only piece of his out here. It was in Ronald Gaines's bedroom. The mirror alone cost four grand when they purchased it." He remained quiet, almost pensive, and she frowned at him. "Lucas?"

He weaved through the jewelry tables and two shelving units stacked with books to get to the mirror. Inching around the beautiful bronze piece, Lucas felt its edges, the front and back like he was searching for something. Finally, he met her gaze. "Peter Gaines put on quite a show out there when I asked if he had any idea who came after you and Ms. Barkley."

"How so?" She withdrew her chicken tender box from the bag, opened it, and nibbled on one. The lukewarm chicken tasted like cardboard in her mouth, and she slid it back in the box.

"He was insulted that we would dare ask if he had anything to do with the attack on you and Ms. Barkley. Basically, we should know better."

"What about my front porch? Did he act surprised about that?"

"I didn't even get that far in my questioning. Jasper told me Peter was belligerent and emotional during his brief phone conversation with them, and that he was highly offended that we'd ever consider he would have anything to do with the attack."

"Isn't that to be expected, whether a person is guilty or innocent?"

"Yes and no. Peter said, 'How dare you accuse me of trying to kill someone.'" He stroked the mirror's side. "Thing is, I never *said* I thought he tried to kill anyone. Just questioned him to see if he might have a connection with the man who did." His phone buzzed. "It's your brother. Stay where I can see you, please."

Lucas paced the front of the store again as he and Jasper spoke. Brielle took a lap around the room, straightening crooked artwork and reorganizing a basket of crocheted hats and gloves on the floor. She ignored the knocked-over table at the front register and far-flung books and toys with careful steps and a bruised heart.

Finally, Lucas came up beside her. "Jasper has a call into the medical examiner about Mr. Gaines. Unfortunately, the ME is on vacation. Returns in two days. He also secured a sampling of essential oils to see if we can narrow down exactly what it is you're smelling on the suspect."

"Do you think that will help the case?"

"Can't hurt to find out as much as possible about this guy. Might provide a lead—or a connection."

"Okay. How is Kinsley?"

"He said she's resting. Didn't seem too worried." He peered past her. "You want to have a look at the back room?"

"If it's okay with you."

"We can look but can't touch."

When they entered the storage room, Brielle's gaze immediately fell upon the large ottoman Shonda had been laying on when she found her yesterday. Goose bumps climbed her arms and legs like a million tiny spiders. She shivered.

He followed her gaze. "That's a Gaines piece?"

"Yes." Her tongue stuck to the roof of her mouth.

"I explained to Peter that any of his father's items stored back here couldn't be touched for at least a week because of the investigation." He stepped ahead of her and pulled out a pair of gloves, then began opening drawers and peering under furniture. "For now, I'd like to check everything you brought over from the mansion. I did yesterday, but today I have a different focus."

While he worked, she went through the small cabinet where she and Shonda kept their purses. Files with receipts and paychecks, sets of old key rings, plus three years of client emails and contracts filled the locked drawers. Shonda had even stored one of her medications inside, which had rolled underneath the files and lodged in the back of the bottom drawer. It must've fallen out of Shonda's purse recently. Brielle grasped the small white bottle and set it near the front of the drawer. Then she pushed back and stood. Cool, stale air washed over her as she circled the room that two days ago, no one except for Shonda, Troy and she had entered. Now it was a police free-for-all, the reminders of her attacker everywhere.

She treaded to the back doors, pushing them open to let in the warm summer air.

"What are you doing?" Lucas called out, crouched in front of an oak dresser.

"It's freezing in here." The storage shed caught her eye out back. The twelve-by-twenty red barn was a miniature of The Antique Depot, with a small AC unit lodged in one of the little side windows.

Except the shed door was ajar.

"Lucas. My shed is open."

He closed a drawer and stood, then came over to look outside.

"I'm certain that was closed and locked yesterday when I left." He stepped outside, turning in a slow circle. "You need cameras installed on the back of the building."

"I've never needed them before. Besides, didn't the guy just damage them?"

"Yes, but there've been plenty of cases where the footage offered clues. I'm going to take a look. Stay close please." He walked past her and through the yard, using the square paver pathway Noah put in for her last year so she didn't have to walk through the mud or dirt.

She hurried after him. He pressed a finger to his mouth, then motioned for her to stand behind one of the shed's open doors. She tucked in behind it, flicking off a cobweb snarled in the corner. Her heart sank. Had Peter Gaines broken into the shed? As far as she knew, nothing from the Gaines mansion had been placed outside. It was all still inside her storage room, except for the mirror in the main part of the store.

She held her breath as Lucas went in the shed. Moments later, he reappeared. "It's clear, but someone must've broken in since we left yesterday."

She slipped out from behind the door and hurried after him. *No.* Her hands flew to her mouth.

Two sets of four-tiered storage shelves lined either side of the interior walls. Normally the old-style milk crates filled with old cookware, kitchen plates and glasses, and other miscellaneous kitchen items were stacked on the left side, while on the right they shelved vintage children's toys, records, and books she hadn't been able to sell but didn't want to get rid of.

Everything had been dumped on the floor, dishes broken, books splayed, crate contents strewn in messy piles that didn't make sense. Kind of like her life.

Lucas started up the car, then drove away from Brielle's store. They were about thirty minutes behind schedule now. But that couldn't be helped.

Watching her crumble to her knees, trying to pick up the chaos after finding the mess inside her storage shed, ignited a dull throbbing pain in his chest. Then he had to be the bad guy and gently pull her out of the shed and remind her not to touch anything, in case there were prints.

Why was Theodore Hardwick doing this to her? What did he want? Lucas's inspection of the furniture from the mansion hadn't offered any hints or clues, though it had been cut short because of the shed. He'd have to come back to finish.

Now they headed to the Gaines mansion. *Finally.* Peter had agreed to an interview at his father's huge home, but he hadn't answered about Stella. Lucas would have to nail her down for an interview, too. He slowed at a stop sign and glanced at Brielle. "You're sure you don't want to go to Jasper and Kinsley's?"

"It's on the other side of town. It would add an hour to your drive and make you late."

"I can work around that."

"I appreciate it, but I'll just come along. In case anything comes up with the items Mr. Donaldson mentioned, at least I'll be there to see them."

"You'll need to stick close to me."

"I will."

He hated the dejection in her tone. Her defeated posture. She reminded him of the colorful, displaced flowers in the pot that had been knocked over on her front porch. She must be feeling as though her life was completely upended. Thank the Lord Jasper and Kinsley were back home, and Kinsley was okay. Per Jasper's message, his wife was on bed rest until she would be induced in two days, so for now they were all at the two-story cabin Jasper and Kinsley shared with Dana Holt.

Brielle was huddled in the seat, arms crossed. Face crumpled and tear-stained. Against his better judgment, he reached over and lay his right palm on her forearm. "Hey, it's going to be okay. We'll find out who's doing this."

She sniffled. "It doesn't feel that way. It feels like nothing will ever be okay again."

"We'll get him," he reiterated. "We know who he is. Just need to catch him." As long as Brielle wasn't part of *that* encounter. He cleared his throat. A change of subject was in order. "Tell me about your favorite read so far this year."

"That's easy. *Jane Eyre*."

"Didn't you read that in high school?"

"Yes. But a client sold me a 1942 hardback edition with a slipcase recently, and I got the urge to reread it. Seeing the beautiful cover reminded me how much I loved the story in high school. So, I bought a contemporary copy and dug in. I'd forgotten all the amazingness that is a Charlotte Brontë book."

"Amazingness, huh." He tucked away his smile, grateful that Brielle's voice had evened out. "What makes the story so amazing?"

"All of it. Have you read it?" He met her eyes briefly, noting her lower lip caught between her teeth.

He placed his focus squarely on the ascending mountain road. "It's a romance. I'd have to turn in my man card if I read that."

"You don't need a card to prove that, Lucas."

He glanced at her, but she had averted her eyes and was staring out the window. Had she just complimented him?

He pulled to a stop sign and looked to his left. "This way?" He hadn't been out near Raven's Peak Mountain in ages.

"Yes. Then the driveway is on the left in about a mile, past the curve in the road."

He accelerated from the stop sign, hugging the outside white line as a large, gold SUV passed on the other side of the road. "What was your favorite part of *Jane Eyre*?"

"The garden scene. I forgot I was reading words."

Garden scene. *Huh*. "Got sucked into the story, then?"

"Very much so."

"Guess that's why it's a classic."

"What was your favorite book this year?" she asked.

He mentally ran through the titles he'd read since January. Work had been busy, with new investigations occurring weekly. Often, he walked through his town house door too exhausted to stay awake, especially after the hard cases. He'd only gotten through a few books so far. "I'd say *The Martian*. I finally got around to reading it and wished I had years ago."

"Sci-fi. I see."

"What's wrong with sci-fi?"

"Nothing. The driveway is up there." She leaned over, pointing. The smell of citrus and fresh air wafted off her hair.

Focus, Scott. Lucas followed her gesture to a large brick-base, black mailbox on the left. It was the only marker of the paved, hidden drive curving up and away from the mountain road.

Lucas had done some research this morning before Brielle woke up. Ronald Gaines had amassed a large sum of money as a builder to the stars in California. Nearly twenty years ago, Mr. Gaines had bought this fifty-five-acre property on the edge of Sumter National Forest, then finally started construction on the mansion about a decade ago. Which explained why Lucas hadn't seen the actual residence yet. He was gone by the time it was built. Plus, the structure was hidden by trees and set at least a third of a mile from the road. Private, just the way Ronald had wanted his home.

"Kind of strange that he built such a huge place way out here," he commented.

"Maybe he wanted to be away from the city," she answered quietly. "You know, away from the crowds."

"Sounds peaceful," Lucas noted as he slowed down. "And lonely."

"Maybe a little."

Jasper had mentioned more than once how he and Noah, and their mom, wished Brielle came around more often for visits and get-togethers.

"At least his family was here, too. Like yours is in Tunnel Creek." He ignored the fact that the Gaines family, for all intents and purposes, appeared quite fractured.

"Yes."

Lucas turned into the driveway and began the upward climb. "Have you been able to see much of your brothers and mom this year?"

"Not as much as they'd like." She angled herself so her knees brushed the passenger-side door. Facing away from him. Saying without words how she felt about this conversation and his insinuation.

"What would *you* like?"

She turned to him with a spark in her eyes. "Did Jasper put you up to this?"

"No." He focused on the narrow, winding driveway. "I'm asking because I'm curious. I care about your family. *All* of you."

"It has taken me years to get to this point, Lucas."

"What? Owning and running your own store?"

"Yes, that. Also working to make sure The Antique Depot has an excellent reputation in the area. Tourists are one thing. They're one and done, you know? Just stop in for trinkets. But many of the antique store owners in the area and this region of the country are tougher to win over. Many of them are at least one generation older than me, so I've had to prove myself. Prove I was here to stay in this business. Earn their respect and their referrals."

"I have no doubt you're respected. You're smart, kind, and level-headed. Plus, it sounds like you've come through for Tunnel Creek residents who have needed particular items."

Her shoulders slumped slightly as he maneuvered around a curve.

"Brielle?"

"The truth is, it hurts to be reminded of him." Her voice hitched on the last word.

He softened his next question. "Who?"

"My dad." She crossed her arms and rubbed her forearms. "Jasper acts like my dad, and Noah looks like him." She sniffed. "They think I don't remember much about Dad because I was only seven when he died. But I do. And worst of all, I still remember that last day like it happened a week ago."

"The day he died?" he prodded gently.

"Yes. Even the moments right before he left. Mom almost went with him, but he urged her to stay to keep an eye on…" She sniffled again. "To keep an eye on me since I'm the youngest."

What could he say? "Isn't that a good thing? That your mom wasn't with him?"

She swiped at a tear. "No. My dad was terrible with directions. He was always getting lost. My mom can locate north, south, east, and west blindfolded and she remembers routes well. If she had been with him…"

"You think he…they wouldn't have gotten lost. That your dad would still be alive."

Brielle was silent, but the heavy, sad tension in the car answered for her. She believed her dad's death could've been stopped if her parents had been together. If her mom hadn't had to stay and watch her. Pieces fell into place. Brielle's somewhat distant relationship with Dana Holt, who was the epitome of grace and love. Her busyness, to keep from focusing on the past.

"I'm sorry. I shouldn't have unloaded that on you now," she whispered.

"It's completely fine. I'm honored that you shared. I hope you know you can always talk to me."

She answered with a noncommittal murmur that made his chest ache. Had she carried this burden since childhood?

Unfortunately, they'd have to pick this conversation up at a later time. The Gaineses' driveway flattened out as it snaked through the trees surrounding Raven's Peak, finally opening up in a manicured, park-like setting that seemed out of place atop the prominent, densely wooded mountaintop.

"It's beautiful up here," he noted. "Like an island on a mountain."

"Wait until you see the house."

A hundred yards later, the palatial brick-and-glass-fronted mansion came into view. Two massive stone chimneys sat at each side of the residence, and green double doors matched the carefully maintained landscaping. A circular brick turret bracketed one side of the house, beside a four-car garage with doors also painted green. The paved drive swept in front of the mansion, then ended in a circular loop in front of the extra-large garage. Two gray, life-size stone statues—a bear and its cub—adorned the side of the house closest to the driveway.

Lucas pulled up near the wide garage and parked.

"You're sure about this?" He fisted the keys. "I can't have you in the room with me when I interview Peter Gaines."

"Speaking of."

The slim-built, brown-haired man from her store parking lot strode through the open garage door, his steps rigid and swift.

"We'll talk more after," Lucas said. "Let me handle him for now."

They climbed out of the vehicle, and Lucas circled the front to stand beside her. He placed himself between Brielle and Mr. Gaines.

"You didn't say we'd have company for the interview." Peter motioned at Brielle, his mouth a straight slash across his face.

Lucas widened his stance and crossed his arms. "She won't be part of the interview. And as far as I know, she has reason to be here. Aidan Donaldson contacted *her* to handle your father's estate items. He specifically asked for Ms. Holt to manage the job."

"I told you before, that was without my permission. Aidan isn't acting in my best interests."

"But Mr. Donaldson *is* the executor of the will, correct?"

Peter's jaw flexed, and he dropped his chin to break eye contact. "He is."

"Until Mr. Donaldson officially tells Ms. Holt to return the items, or you secure documentation from a judge saying otherwise, the items will stay put. Not to mention the ongoing investigation." Lucas glanced at Brielle. "Now, you said you and your sister would do sit-down interviews. Is Stella Gaines here as well?"

Peter scraped a hand through his hair. "Stella went into

town for medication. She suffers from migraines and had to pick up a prescription."

Lucas frowned. "Is she by chance driving a gold SUV?"

"Yes." Peter startled. "You saw her?"

"I did. She drove past us on our way out here." Why had she left? "I wanted to conduct our interview here. With both of you."

"Please. She's very fragile right now. She said I could speak on her behalf."

Lucas buffered a scowl. Stella wasn't a child. What was going on with this family? "Just be aware, she will still need to be interviewed. Soon."

"She already spoke to Officer Holt today."

"A five-minute phone call isn't an interview."

Peter grumbled beneath his breath, then led them inside through the garage. Five minutes later Lucas and he were settled into the high-ceilinged sunroom off the fully-stocked kitchen. His mom would lose her mind in this place. A seamless built-in fridge that would fit at least two bodies, endless granite countertops, an island with an additional sink and cooktop. Two double ovens plus a large wine rack and a coffee bar along the back wall. And the view? Lucas almost whistled when Peter strode through the hallway from the garage and led him back here.

Floor-to-ceiling windows made it feel like they were sitting outside among the trees, on the mountaintop.

Lucas settled into the chair and pulled out his recorder. Today his goal was to ruffle Peter Gaines a bit and try to dig up more information about him and Stella and any possible connection to Theodore Hardwick. Brielle was situated in the living room at the front of the house, chatting with a client on the phone.

He matched Peter's strident frown. "Let's get started."

SEVEN

"Yes, Helen, I'm okay." Brielle wandered away from the living room, the small black burner phone set to her ear. She'd called her longtime friend and client, Helen Thomasino, to let her know she wouldn't be able to complete Helen's order of an eight-piece Cumberland Brambleberry stoneware dinner set until the investigation was complete.

Brielle reassured Helen that she was safe and the sweet widow's items were intact. She promised Helen she'd call once the investigation was closed and the store reopened. Then she disconnected the call and looked around. She stood near the front door, on the side of the large foyer, and the distant rumble of the two men's voices followed her. Lucas's low and steady, Peter's higher-pitched and inconsistent. They were very different men.

She stepped into the hallway to her left, searching for a restroom to freshen up. If she wasn't mistaken, this was the way to Ronald Gaines's master suite. Memories of the heated conversation between Peter and Stella assaulted her. The looks on their faces. The anger in the room. Surely, she hadn't imagined that. And today, Stella left right before they arrived.

Strange. What happened between them? Was it just about their father's things, or was there something else going on?

When Lucas asked after Stella, Peter seemed to be protecting her. At least, it came across that way.

Brielle moseyed down the hallway, studying the artwork and unique décor. The mansion was well-turned out but not overdone. Ronald Gaines must've hired an interior designer with a flair for color. She peeked into a room—an office, it appeared. Wall-to-wall bookshelves crowded the plush space, and the window faced the driveway. Through the sheer curtains, she noticed their borrowed, unmarked car parked outside.

Brielle retreated from the room and continued down the hall. There. The next room was a half bath. She slipped inside, turning on the faucet at the pedestal sink to splash a little cool water on her face. Her thoughts shifted to the drive here. Why had she told Lucas about her dad? He'd been through his own trauma and didn't need to know all the Holt family secrets.

"*My* secrets," she whispered to the silver, scalloped mirror. Jasper and Noah didn't even know.

Lucas had been so gentle with her in the car. Caring and sensitive. Understanding. The cute teenager she'd crushed on years ago had turned into a thoughtful man. And handsome. Those wire-rimmed glasses only accentuated his thickly lashed, blue eyes.

Her cheeks turned rosy remembering what she said to him about his man card comment. *You don't need a card to prove that, Lucas.*

"Stop it, Brielle. He's not interested, remember?" She flicked off the light and left the bathroom, peering to her left then right. Did she dare go near the master suite again?

The burner cell buzzed in her pocket. She retrieved it and read, then reread the text.

This is Aidan Donaldson. Peter texted and told me you're at the house with Agent Scott. There are more items boxed up in the basement I wanted you to look over. Also are you able to price his fossil collection? I return later tonight. We can discuss soon.

Lucas said the interview might take forty-five minutes to an hour. What if she took a brief look in the basement to assess the items? Then at least she'd have an idea of what was left.

She crossed the foyer with quick steps, sweeping past the double doors, then proceeded to the hallway on the other side of the house. A large brown door on the right caught her eye. She tried the knob and found it unlocked. Opening it wide, Brielle saw the well-lit staircase leading downstairs.

Bingo. The basement.

She glanced back across the foyer toward the kitchen and sunroom. Lucas was nearby, Mr. Donaldson was on his way back here, Peter was occupied, and Stella had left shortly before they arrived. Her desire to see what else Ronald Gaines had collected during his lifetime consumed her.

Would it hurt to take a quick look?

She pushed aside her uncertainty and padded down the carpeted stairs, then turned right, her mind spinning as the large space opened up. It was a long basement, with high windows and tan carpet throughout. A pair of closed glass doors held what looked like a workout room with a rowing machine and a treadmill. Black free weights were neatly lined up under a window. The rest of the basement—as far as she could see—contained high windows that opened up to the beautiful view of the mountain, and near the back of the space sat a couple more doors. More rooms? Incredible. The basement was easily larger than her twelve-hundred-square-foot bungalow.

She stepped past two dark wood, built-in bookshelves set beneath a brick archway, ignoring the urge to peruse the books. If she was ultimately allowed to sell any more of the Gaineses' items, she'd look then. But that was a big *if* should Peter Gaines get his way.

Bronze wall sconces gave off dim yellow light as she approached the far end of the basement. Heavy, masculine leather furniture surrounded a glass-top coffee table in front of a huge flat-screen TV hung over a distressed wood entertainment center, and a pool table filled the other side of the room. In between the couches and pool table, a waist-high silver refrigerator set against the wall. Empty bottles of water and soda overflowed a trash can beside it, and a thick blanket wadded up beside a misshapen pillow. Did someone sleep down here? On the glass-top coffee table, a discarded soda can sat atop a coaster, next to an empty bag of pretzels and a crushed fast-food bag.

If they didn't sleep down here, someone must've spent time in the basement recently.

Her gaze swept the rest of the area. To the left, two doors beckoned. One glass, one solid wood. Through the glass door, a dozen or more shiny black, gray, and tan objects caught her attention. What were those? She edged closer, her eyes widening.

Incredible. Ronald Gaines had a huge fossil collection. Her contact at the American Museum of Natural History in New York would lose her mind.

Several shelves were propped along the walls, filled to the brim with what looked like jaw bones, leg bones, and a wide variety of smaller rocks and stone fossils. Two tables sat in the middle of the room, more stone-like items atop their surfaces. White gloves, a microscope, and a magnifying glass sat in the center of the table. The microscope looked heavy—and expensive.

A distant *creak* sent a prickle of awareness over her limbs. She whirled around, looking toward the stairs. But they were behind the brick arch and bookshelves. Had the creaking sound come from the ceiling? She'd only been down here two or three minutes. Maybe one of the men was walking around upstairs?

The rumors about the Backyard Bandit flashed in her mind like a blinking billboard at night. She inched backward, until she pressed against the wall in between the room with the fossil collection and the other mysterious room. How could she get out if not by the stairs? She'd had enough of strangers coming after her and shouldn't have come down here alone.

Stupid. She should've waited for Lucas.

She looked around. Another double set of doors was situated a dozen feet away, thicker and heavier than inside doors. Two locks designated them as outside entry. But to get to them, she had to make it all the way across the large lounging area where the pool table and couches sat.

If someone *had* come downstairs, they'd spot her.

A chuffing noise stopped then started, similar to the sound of her own shoes as she'd treaded over the carpet this way. *That* wasn't upstairs.

A shiver careened down her spine.

She snatched a pool cue stick from the wall rack and backtracked until her shoulder blades bumped into the closed, wood door. What was inside this room? As quietly as possible, Brielle gripped the door handle and turned. It gave way, then she slunk inside the dark space, gripping the cue stick. Were there no windows in this room?

She closed the door and felt along the wall. Might be better to leave the lights off anyway. Brielle slid in until she hit what felt like a metal dividing wall. No, that was a filing cabinet. And another. She inched farther. As her eyes adjusted to the darkness, she noticed a large cabinet on the far wall and a desk. Atop the desk sat an extra-wide computer screen, flanked by a half dozen or so smaller screens on the side and above. Was this a security room? She knew there'd be cameras here, but an actual security room?

Did Lucas know about this?

She peered past the desk. Under the lone, high, narrow window, a twin bed was thrown on the floor, a twisted off-white sheet on the top.

Someone slept down here?

Icy fingertips climbed her spine as she slipped farther inside and held still. At least she was hidden behind the stacked filing cabinets and had the cue stick. She drew in a couple of deep breaths, trying to calm down and listen for any more sounds. Instead, the strong scent of body odor and something else filled her nostrils and gagged her.

Her mouth fell open.

The same pungent scent she noted in her store was here, too. Lucas had told her to use her senses when he asked her to go over what happened that morning. And she was.

This was the same smell. She was sure of it.

She had to text Lucas. He would have no idea where she was in this monstrous home. He might search outside because he knew she wasn't excited to be back inside. She slipped out her phone and pulled up his number, then started tapping out a text.

Basement. Help.

Her foot collided with a soft, material lump. Was it clothes? No, it felt harder than that. She reached down, her fingers groping the floor. A purse.

Her chest caved in. Was that the purse she'd borrowed from Lucas's mom that was taken at Long's Lumber?

"What're you doing in here?"

A man's voice came out of the shadows near the door. Brielle screamed and flung the purse toward him. Her phone fell from her grasp.

He slapped away the purse and grabbed for her. Her head slammed into the wall as she clawed away from him, a throb filling her skull and dimming her vision.

Where was the cue stick? His hand pawed at her shoulders, catching her hair. Pain burned her scalp when he jerked on it. She shouted and kicked out, her foot catching him in the upper thigh. He grunted and fell backward into the desk chair, which flew toward the bed from his momentum, giving her a moment to push past for the door. She snatched the thin wooden pool stick and was halfway through the opening when he caught her again, yanking her arm back.

"Let go of me!" Brielle twisted away, and the cue stick slipped from her grasp. *No.*

"Get back here."

Where was her phone? Still in the storage room? Were the outside entry doors unlocked? She darted for the doors, the man growling after her.

A brick bookend caught her eye, and she snatched it from the end table then turned to smash it in her attacker's face. But she only managed to hit the side of his throat. He let out a curse and batted away the brick.

She turned and ran toward the doors. The staircase was too far away. He'd catch her. She screamed again as he caught up, his arms everywhere, yanking forcefully so she stalled mid-stride. No. She couldn't let this happen.

Please, God. Give me a way out.

The man rolled her to the ground and kneeled on her rib cage. He wore a mask, just like at her store, but his flat, hard brown eyes glared down at her. "You're not getting away this time, sweetheart."

"Don't call me that." A sob built in her chest as he crushed her with his weight and held her shoulders to the carpet.

He straddled her, his heavy frame pressing on her ribs. "I'll call you whatever I want to call you. Now the thing is, sweetheart, we need the—"

Brielle raised her knee like Jasper had taught her when he became an officer, flexing her hips side to side in order to unseat him. Her knee came up hard against his backbone, and he leaned over her. She rammed her elbow—the strongest point on her body, Jasper said—into the man's throat. It grazed the skin and landed on his chin. He groaned and fell forward. She lurched upright and darted toward the doors, her pulse drumming in her ears.

The sound of the man moaning and trying to move behind her sent her flying. A quick flick unlocked the dead bolt, then she shoved the door open. Blinding sunlight poured into the dimly lit basement, and she burst out of the building.

"Lucas!" she screamed, her eyes watering from the bright light.

A long, narrow greenhouse filled the clearing on the side of the mansion ahead. The mansion's front doors would be all the way around the large home. She wouldn't make it. The man would catch her. Could she hide in the greenhouse? Would there be someone in there to ask for help? Or tools for protection?

She surged away from the basement doors, her legs tottering like a newborn colt's. Beyond the greenhouse, the woods capped the mountainside in a sea of green. She couldn't risk running into the woods. He'd catch her and she'd be too far away from Lucas.

Brielle reached the greenhouse and yanked open the glass doors. Humid air knocked into her as she shut the door and stumbled inside. Plants and flowers lined the shelves down the center of the warm interior. She dashed down the row, desperately looking for any tool she could use against her attacker. She snatched a wooden-handled trowel the size of her forearm and crouched behind a shelf, her chest heaving.

Had the man gone the other way?

The stark sound of breaking glass answered her question. "You think I can't find you? Wrong. And I'm sick of chasing after you. Let's finish this."

She peered around the plants just as he stepped into the center of the greenhouse aisle. His angry, determined movements sent her heart tumbling into her shoes. He flung his arm out, knocking over a few of the potted annuals. Leaves, dirt, and plastic pots scattered all over the ground.

"Police! Put your hands up."

Lucas's shout interrupted the chaos, coming from behind her attacker. Brielle's knees buckled as Lucas barreled out of the basement doors in the background, his gun drawn.

"Put your hands in the air!" Lucas repeated.

The man muttered a curse, then backtracked out of the greenhouse door. He dashed downhill toward the woods. Brielle clutched the trowel. "Lucas!"

"Stay there," he shouted as he ran past.

Peter Gaines scurried out of the basement doors like a roach shunning sunlight. "What's going on? What are you doing in my greenhouse?"

"Trying to stay alive," she yelled, gripping the trowel, then moved toward the door, eyeing Peter. "I thought this was your father's greenhouse?"

"No." His expression hardened. "My father was never

interested in plants. Now you want to tell me what is going on out here? Who broke my door?"

"Why don't you tell me? Because someone just tried to kill me in your basement."

Lucas crashed through the woods downhill from the Gaines mansion for two or three minutes then pulled up short, his chest heaving. No sign of the man. No doubt this was the guy they were looking for. *Was* Theodore Hardwick the Backyard Bandit? He removed his glasses and swiped the sweat from his brows, then doubled back to the greenhouse to check on Brielle. She must be terrified. While he was fairly certain Peter Gaines wasn't capable of actual murder, he didn't want Brielle alone with him longer than necessary.

He'd been in the middle of the interview with Peter when his phone pinged. Her short, desperate text lit a fire beneath his feet. After demanding Peter tell him where the door to the basement was, Lucas ran down the stairs to the tune of Brielle's screams. A split-second check of the rooms down there led him to the open doors, where he'd come upon a man entering the greenhouse and Brielle huddled on the other side of the glass structure.

Lucas's jaw clenched as he jogged back up to the mansion's side yard. He checked the greenhouse, but she wasn't inside.

"Brielle!" he shouted, looking around. No answer. He took off around the garage. The driveway came into view, and there was Brielle, hunched over beside the white Charger, visibly shaken.

And there was Peter Gaines, standing much too close to her.

"Hey, Brielle, are you alright?" He rushed over.

"Lucas." She straightened and ran to meet him, folding

into his embrace as easily as breathing. Trembling like a leaf in a thunderstorm.

"I don't know what you people think is going on, but this has nothing to do with me," Peter snarled. "She said someone came after her. Well, what's she doing traipsing all over my house? I don't know who he is or what he's doing. It's probably that Backyard Bandit the news keeps talking about. Put that on the record."

"No one is charging you with anything—yet." Lucas leveled him with a glare over Brielle's head. "Did you see the suspect, then? The man who went after Ms. Holt?"

"No, I did not." Peter crossed his arms.

"Then you don't *know* if you know him or not."

Peter narrowed his eyes. "You're trying to catch me in some kind of confession, but that's not going to work. Despite what you people keep insinuating, I haven't hired a hit man for…for her." He jabbed a finger at Brielle. "I have more important things to do with my time."

Lucas disentangled gently from Brielle, setting her beside him, keeping one arm around her shoulders as he addressed Peter. "I'll be with you in a minute to take your statement. I'll also need to search the basement. Right now, I need to speak to Ms. Holt. Alone."

"What about me? This is my family's house. Now some man is down there in my basement? What about *my* safety?"

"Ms. Holt is the victim right now, Mr. Gaines."

"Don't call me that. My father is Mr. Gaines."

Lucas shoved his free hand in his pocket so he wasn't tempted to punch the guy. "I'll be inside shortly. Please wait by the front doors."

"We have to do this again?"

"We weren't done." Lucas directed a warning look at the man. Peter stalked off toward the front doors, and Lucas turned back to Brielle. The welling of protectiveness and anger had shocked him when he saw the man standing in the greenhouse doorway, a knife clutched in his hands. Knowing Brielle was the target of his attack.

Lucas stood in front of her and softly clasped her wrists. "Hey, talk to me." She didn't pull away, and in fact seemed to press closer to him, her features frozen in shock.

"It was him. The man from my store."

He nodded. "I figured as much."

"He had the same weird, pungent odor." She shivered, and Lucas fought the urge to pull her against him again. It wasn't professional, these feelings. Because the thought of that man touching or hurting her kindled a dangerous flame in his chest that Lucas hadn't felt since he'd had to help identify Leah years ago.

"I'm sorry. I should've made you stay right there in the kitchen." He looked around for Peter, but the man had disappeared. Must be inside. Lucas slipped his glasses off and rubbed the bridge of his nose before setting them back in place.

He'd gotten little out of Peter during the interview, other than complaints and the same alibi he had already given Jasper, along with a clear-eyed denial that he had anything to do with the attack on Brielle and Shonda yesterday or the bomb on Brielle's porch. However, Lucas had uncovered a deep-seated animosity toward Aidan Donaldson, as well as more of that peculiar protectiveness toward Stella. Almost like Peter was shielding her from something. But what?

"You don't need to apologize, Lucas. It was a stupid decision to listen to Aidan. I should've waited for you."

He stared down at her. "What?"

"Mr. Donaldson texted me while you and Peter were speaking. He mentioned there were boxed-up items in the basement, and he wanted me to look at Mr. Gaines's fossil collection."

"How did he get your number?"

"I texted him at the restaurant, remember? Also, it sounds like Peter texted him that we were here, as well."

"Right." Lucas pressed his mouth into a straight line. Aidan Donaldson was digging himself into a deep hole. "Do you have your phone?"

"No." She groaned and closed her eyes. "I dropped it when the man came after me. It's probably still in that room." She shivered, reopening them. "It looked like that man—or someone—lives down there. There was a bed and… Oh! The purse you lent me that was your mom's? It's in that room."

Lucas shook his head. Was someone living in the mansion basement? Hopefully, prints on the leather would identify who'd chased them and stolen the purse from the lumberyard. It had to all tie to Theodore Hardwick. But was he then tied to someone at this estate?

Lucas filed the questions and details into a mental notebook that was quickly filling up.

"As soon as another officer arrives, you're going with them and I'm searching the basement for evidence. Where was the purse?"

She explained about the cameras and security room, along with what else she'd seen downstairs. "Mr. Gaines has an amazing fossil collection. It must be worth a fortune."

And that was likely the heart of the issue here. The family must be battling it out for the right to sell—or keep, in Peter Gaines's case—these items. But that didn't answer why Theodore was going after Brielle. She must have something he wanted.

She continued. "When I talked to Mr. Donaldson before I came here the first time, he seemed distracted, but not rude or short, the way Peter Gaines comes across. Mr. Donaldson doesn't seem capable of being…part of this." She sent the mansion a dark look.

"People are often not what they seem." He'd learned that the hard way through the years. "Your brother found that out, too. Wasn't it Dean Hammond who betrayed him and the Tunnel Creek PD, with those weapons they found in the Whisper Mountain Tunnel?"

"Yes, that's true." She rubbed her neck, lifting her hair in the process. A red scratch caught his eye. He leaned close, shifting stray hairs away from her neck and throat to inspect the small laceration. Her soft inhalation made him pause, and he turned so their faces were only inches apart.

"Lucas?"

"There's a..." His tongue stuck to the roof of his mouth. "You have a small scratch. It's not bleeding much but will need to be cleaned and bandaged."

Her lovely hazel eyes swept over his face, and he backed up to put some space between them. This wasn't going to work. Because being around Brielle Holt was wrecking his focus on this investigation. Jasper had enough to worry about. He would *not* want Lucas involved with Brielle, Lucas was certain of that. Once this case was solved and she was safe, he'd return to Myrtle Beach and get on with his life. "I'm going to ask the officer to take you to the ER."

"Are you coming along?"

"Can't. I have to stay here."

"I don't think I need to go to the hospital again."

"Please. I want to make sure you're okay. Then you can go to Jasper's place tonight while I work." He had evidence to search for here, evidence to sort through at the station, pictures to study, calls to make.

She motioned toward the house and Peter Gaines, inside now. "You can't arrest him?"

"Unfortunately, no, there's nothing I can charge him with at this point. Unless I find items in the basement with his fingerprints, which would implicate him. I'll be contacting a judge to get a warrant to search this property and check those security cameras. I think we may also need to consult with a forensic accountant to make sure the Gaines heirs aren't hiding any financial information."

The other officer pulled up the long drive. Lucas offered a brief wave, then turned to Brielle. "Please, go to the ER. I'll text Jasper and update him."

She gazed at him with a pensive expression, then wrapped her arms around his waist and fit her face between his shoulder and neck. He forgot everything he'd just mentally filed away as soon as she leaned into him, the light, clean scent of oranges filling his mind.

He closed his eyes for a moment. "Wait a minute." They popped open.

She pulled back. "What is it?"

"I wonder if our guy Theodore wears patchouli oil. I worked with another officer who wore it. Strong stuff. I didn't like it, either. I'll get those samples and send them home with Jasper."

"Okay." She nodded. "Be careful, Lucas."

"Always." He quoted a particularly emotional line from a popular fantasy series he knew she'd read, because he'd asked her to read it in high school. They'd talked about it for weeks afterward, and today, her face transformed into a beautiful smile at the simple word.

Then she turned and walked toward the other officer, and Lucas beelined for the mansion's front doors. He needed to figure out why Brielle had become the target of this dangerous criminal.

And make sure she didn't become the target of his heart in the meantime.

EIGHT

"The baby is kicking?" Brielle asked Kinsley.

Her petite sister-in-law sprawled across the smaller couch in the cabin living room, her face contorted with another contraction. "Yes. She's very active. I think I'm in trouble."

"Sounds like baby girl will keep Jasper on his toes."

Meanwhile *she* was off her toes. Trying to relax at Jasper and Kinsley's cabin, as her mom and brothers asked her to. But her mind kept returning to Lucas and what happened earlier.

Brielle spent a blessedly brief hour in the ER undergoing basic tests and having her knife wound from yesterday checked and rebandaged, only to be told she was the healthiest patient the doctor had seen all day and to go home. *If only I could go home.* Instead, she'd ridden with Jasper back to his cabin because Lucas was working. Either at the Gaines estate or at the station. She wasn't sure.

"No doubt baby will keep us both busy." Kinsley gave a funny little smile and shifted her position. "Oh, she's on the move again. Want to feel?" She lifted Brielle's palm and settled it on her burgeoning belly.

Small but definite taps pushed against Brielle's palm. Tiny, insistent. Her throat thickened, and tears unexpectedly prickled her eyes. Miraculous new life. "I can feel her."

"Pretty amazing, isn't it?" Kinsley offered another grin, her long, strawberry-blond hair tumbling over her shoulders.

Jasper's wildlife biologist wife moved Brielle's hand with precise motions so Brielle's palm matched up to the sweet little bumps and wiggles occurring inside her swelling midsection.

"It is amazing."

Kinsley balanced Jasper's boisterousness with her calm, matter-of-fact demeanor, while adding color to her brother's life—often in the form of critters. She and Gabe, Jasper's son from his first marriage, had acquired a garden of milkweed plants and wildflowers out back. Beautiful butterflies and busy bees flitted around the cabin and yard during spring and summer.

"Tell me how you're feeling." Kinsley's eye contact was direct and tender, cutting right through any social pleasantries Brielle would've tried to pawn on her.

"Oh, you know, just peachy." She drew her hand back, gingerly touching the knife wound on her side. "I don't want to upset you with details."

"You won't. I want you to talk about it."

Out in the yard, a chorus of barking carried through the windows. Someone must've arrived.

"You've been through a lot, Brielle. I know what that's like." She grimaced. "Life getting turned upside down and you can't catch your breath."

"It's been a whirlwind, that's for sure." With all that was happening, what bothered her most right now was being away from Lucas. Wondering how and what he was doing. If he was okay. Had he left the Gaines mansion yet? The memory of him holding her close after the attack clung to her thoughts like a toddler to its mother's legs.

She nibbled on her nail so Kinsley wouldn't be able to read her thoughts.

"Lucas seems like such a nice guy," Kinsley said slowly. "Jasper told me about his fiancée before our wedding. It's kind of like the loss of my parents." Her mouth curved upside down with sadness. "You never get over it, but with God's grace, you can keep living, even with joy."

Brielle nodded. "Lucas seems to find healing in his job. At least, he's mentioned that it helped after he lost Leah. We mostly talk about this investigation, though. Trying to figure out what's going on." She gave a quick smile. "And books."

"Books? Fun. Which ones?" Kinsley's gaze roamed over Brielle's face.

"Aunt Bee!"

The inside entry garage door slammed shut, and Gabriel sprinted down the hall toward her. Leo and Mike, redbone coonhounds, trailed at his heels, their nails clicking on the wood floors. Trek, a retired K9 deputy Jasper adopted—along with Dash—all followed. The ruckus saved her from answering Kinsley's perceptive questions about Lucas.

Brielle's sweet, freckled nephew—growing so fast he was all arms and legs—careened toward her like a child-sized tornado. She stood quickly and caught him, then stepped away from the couch and spun him in circles, ignoring the sting on her side. Their laughter tangled up in a chorus of exuberant noise that almost erased all the awful events of the last two days.

"More, more!" Gabe begged when she finally stopped.

"Gabe, Aunt Bee has had a rough day." Kinsley warned. "Give her some space, buddy."

"It's okay." She set Gabe down and inspected him, cupping his bony shoulders and ruffling his hair. "Spinning in circles makes me feel like a kid again. Whew." She hugged him to her once more. "You've gotten so big! You're at least a foot taller than my last visit."

"He's trying to keep up with the caterpillars in our garden," Kinsley teased.

"Yeah, they're growing in their pupils."

Kinsley tweaked Gabe's side. "Pew-pahs," she corrected gently. "The caterpillars turn into butterflies in their *pupas*. A pupil is the black circle in your eyes that helps you see sunlight."

Gabe opened his eyes wide and blinked at Brielle like he was testing his pupils out.

"Your mom is so smart." Brielle made her eyes big, too.

While Kinsley wasn't Gabe's biological mom, she'd become his adoptive mom soon after she and Jasper married. Despite fighting envy about Kinsley's tight relationship with her mom, Brielle was grateful for Jasper's wife and her place in their family.

Gabe wrapped his skinny arms around her waist. "I missed you, Aunt Bee."

Her heart softened and her eyes stung at his sweet, sincere words. His guileless affection always overwhelmed her. Because she'd been that way once, too. Before Dad's death. Before they'd moved back to the states and started over, minus her beloved father.

Being around family, even all these years later, always brought her back to that place of loss. Pain. Grief. The deep longing for what once was. And being here resurrected the guilt, because only she knew she bore a major part in their family's loss.

Tonight, though, didn't feel as heavy as in the past. She considered her conversation with Lucas on the drive to the Gaines estate earlier. It almost seemed that while revealing her heartache to him, his empathy and her honesty had somehow mended the hidden wounds in her heart. Just a little.

"I'm sorry I haven't seen you in a while, buddy." She

squeezed her eyes shut as he fit up against her, his head pressed to her heart. After a few moments, she opened them to find Lucas, Noah, and Jasper standing in the hallway, watching her and Gabe.

"Lucas?" She held on to Gabe and tried to keep the pleased surprise from her voice. "Didn't you have work to do on the case?"

"I did some, then your brother strong-armed me into coming for a late dinner. I'll head back to the station after." He held her gaze steadily, and her stomach flip-flopped.

"Auntie Bee, we get to do the maze at the fair, right?" Gabe broke away from her embrace and looked up at her.

"Gabriel," Jasper said. "I'm not sure the fair is a good idea right now."

"Aw, man." Gabe collapsed onto the couch beside Kinsley like a balloon deflated by a pin. "But I wanted to do a race through the maze."

"Gabriel, Aunt Brielle has had a hard week. Remember? We're not sure that will work out. I'm sorry." Kinsley tousled his hair.

Brielle sank to the edge of the couch, too. She'd completely forgotten about promising Gabe she'd bring him along to help at her booth at the county fair this weekend.

"I need to go check on the burgers." Jasper spoke to the room, but met Brielle's gaze, his brows arched in question. "Gabe, I need your help."

"Oh-kay." Gabe followed his dad down the hallway, and the pack of dogs trailed the little boy. Moments later the back door opened and shut. Dana Holt appeared, two baking mitts engulfing her hands. Brielle attempted to smile at her mom, but instead, out of nowhere, tears threatened. She looked down at her lap, blinking them away.

"Anyone want to help me with the brownies? Brielle? Lucas?"

"I'll help. I don't like sitting still all the time. I know, I'll be careful." Kinsley stood and lumbered toward her mother-in-law. "Gabe will be okay not going to the fair with you." She patted Brielle's shoulder as she walked by. "We just want you safe."

"I'm sorry…" She exhaled, and it sounded too much like a sob. "Thank you."

"I echo that sentiment," her mom called out. "The fair will be there next year."

Brielle tried again to smile. She watched Kinsley waddle down the hall to join her mom, leaving her alone in the cabin living room with unpredictable emotions and Lucas standing quietly nearby.

"May I join you?"

"Of course." She motioned at the couch, then noticed a dark brown crumb near his mouth. "Looks like Mom already passed out a couple brownies." She grinned, then reached over and plucked the tiny piece of chocolate from below his lips. When she met his eyes, their faces were only inches apart. Her heartbeat faltered, then sped up.

"Someone needed to taste test the first batch of brownies, and I volunteered."

"Ah, tough gig."

They grinned at each other, and the space between them shrank. Prickles of awareness warmed her cheeks and neck. She rubbed her throat. "Did you find anything out at the station?"

"We did." His smile faded. "I searched the house. Got this." He pulled her burner phone out and handed it to her. "I copied your texts from Mr. Donaldson. Found the purse in that back room. We're running the prints now. The tracks I saw around the greenhouse match the tracks I saw at your house and at the fast-food place. Expensive shoes."

Shoes that had chased after her. She shivered.

Lucas continued. "After I checked inside, I searched the grounds one more time. Found a path in the woods, opposite the driveway."

"So Theodore Hardwick might be the Backyard Bandit?"

"Very possible."

"Why would he have killed Mr. Gaines? And why is he after me?"

"I'm wondering if he broke into the mansion the night Mr. Gaines was in the basement. Then Theodore killed him. And maybe there's a particular piece from the items at the mansion he wants, and he believes you have it." He shook his head. "I need that autopsy report from the medical examiner to at least pin down cause of death."

"I don't understand how Peter and Stella were clueless about someone living down there."

"Possibly because they don't live there year-round. They may be gone a lot. Because Peter was with me today, and he has an alibi for the other situations, he's still free. We have his prints, so if they're on the purse, we'll know. Add to that the fact that Aidan Donaldson texted you and basically urged you down to the basement."

"I can't believe Mr. Donaldson would be part of this." She paused. "What about Stella Gaines? Where was she?"

"I already checked. She went into town, picking up groceries and a prescription like Peter said. I even checked with the pharmacist."

"You think Aidan Donaldson wanted me down there and sent Theodore after me?"

"I don't know." He ran his palms along his jeans. "In law enforcement, the most logical explanation usually proves true. But, of course, there's human nature. It's unpredictable, subject to whims and emotions and other things. In this case, it appears family secrets shape what's going on. We need to get to the bottom of what this family is hiding." He turned to her. "So, what's this about the county fair and Gabe?"

She grabbed one of the American flag pillows on the couch and set it over her lap, then pictured Kinsley's cute pregnant belly and feeling Kinsley and Jasper's sweet little girl moving. Painful longing lodged in her chest, working up into her throat.

"Brielle?"

She shook away the unexpected yearning. "The fair. So, every summer I have a booth at the county fair. I bring some of the smaller items from my store. Books, knick-knacks, costume jewelry, dishes. Mom makes some type of unique treat to hand out. It's a fun weekend. A few months ago, I promised Gabe I'd let him come along and we'd see the animals. I said we'd time ourselves in the maze to see if we could finish fastest. There's a prize for that each year."

"That's nice of you to include him."

She squished the pillow between her palms. "What now? Do I cancel? I've already paid for the booth, and Troy was going to help me load items in my trailer Friday afternoon."

"I need to talk to Jasper about it. The case is very much still active. A fair is a bustling place. Lots of people."

"I know." She leaned her head back on the couch, and their shoulders bumped, arms mingling. "I just hate letting Gabe down."

"I understand. Let's see what transpires over the next day or so. I'm interviewing Mr. Donaldson tomorrow morning. That should shed some light on things. I have calls out to multiple places about the investigation. I'll talk to Jasper about the fair. For now, I have another important question for you."

"What is it?"

"Tell me more about this garden scene."

"The garden scene? Oh, right. *Jane Eyre*. So, Jane and

Mr. Rochester are finally talking. Really talking, after circling around each other for weeks. And their words…" She sighed. "They bicker so romantically."

"Romantic bickering?" He guffawed. "I believe that's the exact definition of oxymoron."

She dug her elbow lightly into his ribs. "No, it's deliciously romantic." A yawn broke over her words, so long and loud she slapped her hand over her mouth.

"Sounds like you need to eat, then get some sleep. It's been quite a day."

"It has. And going to sleep soon sounds good." She closed her eyes for a moment, wishing she could erase the images of the last two days. But then she realized that included her time spent with Lucas, and her heart gave a lurch. As stressful and scary as it had been, she wouldn't trade their deep conversations or the quiet time with him. "I doubt my mom would appreciate me finally coming over, then going to bed early."

"I think your mom wants whatever is best for you. And as far as what you shared earlier today, about your dad, I can't imagine she blames you." Lucas wore a solemn expression. No longer teasing. "She loves you, no matter what happened when you were a child."

His blue eyes bore into hers, and she wondered what he looked like without his glasses on. She'd only caught little glimpses here and there when he adjusted them. She reached over and gently pulled them off. He held perfectly still except for a small crease between his brows.

And it hit her, the bold thing she'd just done. Carefully, she replaced them on his face and prayed he didn't see her pulse thumping wildly in her temple or neck.

"Something the matter with my glasses?"

"I, ah, wanted to see what you look like without your glasses on. You know, Clark Kent and all."

He chuckled, but it sounded forced. "And what do I look like?"

"You look like Lucas."

"Is that okay?" Once again, their faces were only inches apart.

"Absolutely," she whispered.

His phone buzzed from his pocket. Resignation weighed his voice down. "Hold on."

His brows gathered in a frown as he read the text. "Prints came back a match. Now we just need to catch Mr. Hardwick."

"Burgers are ready. Come get your sides," her mom called from the kitchen. Lucas stood, then offered Brielle a hand up. She grasped his, jolting at the warmth and contact, then let go as soon as she was standing. Lucas hadn't been interested in her back then, and he wasn't now. He'd already admitted coming back to Tunnel Creek was painful, that it made him think of Leah. His work was across the state.

And *she* needed to keep her emotions under control.

Because with all that was going on, adding these growing feelings for a man who wasn't staying around—and wasn't interested in her that way—could prove dangerous, too.

Lucas stretched his arms above his head in Jasper's chair. He sat at his friend's work desk, trying to pinpoint Theodore Hardwick's connection to the Gaines family. The suspect's expensive shoes were sold in multiple high-end, mall department stores from California to New York City. Four hundred and forty-six pairs were sold in the last two years. Combing through the list of buyers would be tedious work. Not to mention, what if he'd stolen them from the Gaineses' home? And both patchouli oil and cologne were increasingly offered through essential oil dealers as well as grocery stores nationwide to help with dry skin, acne, and even as an antibacterial agent.

"Those are long shots, Dash," he murmured to his snoring office mate.

Dash whined softly on the dog bed in his crate in the corner. Jasper remained a few doors down, filling out paperwork for his paternity leave.

It was nearly nine a.m. Lucas had stayed at the station until midnight, then headed back to his parents' condo for a painfully brief six hours of sleep. Brielle had spent the night at Jasper and Kinsley's cabin, then Jasper had brought Brielle to the station this morning so she could give her statement about the attack at the Gaines mansion.

Aidan Donaldson was expected to arrive any moment.

Lucas let go of the mouse and downed the last of his cold coffee. Why did the thought of seeing Brielle again make his mouth dry and his pulse race? Dash lifted his head, his intelligent brown eyes watching Lucas. Those large, triangular ears were no doubt tuned to his handler down the hall.

Footsteps treaded toward them, and Dash cocked his head.

Brielle appeared in the doorway. "Hey."

Their gazes connected, and his chest warmed more than it should at the sight of her. She looked rested, her wavy brown hair loose around her lovely face.

He considered—briefly—their hug at the Gaines mansion and their conversation yesterday at Jasper and Kinsley's cabin. He had always enjoyed being around her in high school, found her fun and easy to talk to. But now? Now it felt like he was a moth and she the light he was drawn to.

And that wasn't going to work. No doubt, she didn't want that—and neither would Jasper. She'd hugged him yesterday because she'd been scared out of her wits. That was it.

"Hey, how'd it go?" he forced out.

"I'd prefer not to have to give another statement again. Ever, in my entire life."

"Understandable. You want to sit?"

"If I'm not interrupting anything."

"Nope. I need a brain break." *And I just like having you around. Too much.*

She wandered closer, then sank into the lone chair beside the desk. "What are you up to?"

"Checking on the suspect's shoes. Researching patchouli oil and looking up where it's sold around here. Trying to find a connection between Theodore Hardwick and Stella, Peter, or Mr. Donaldson."

"Speaking of—isn't Mr. Donaldson coming in?"

Lucas nodded, glancing at the clock on the desk. "Any minute now. Should be interesting."

"He's very formal, from what I remember from our phone calls."

"Thanks. I'll keep that in mind." He tried not to stare at the generous shape of her mouth as she smiled. *Cut it out, Scott.* "How'd you sleep last night?"

"I'm pretty sure I was out before my head hit the pillow, so I take that as a positive. Oh, have you gotten any updates on Shonda?"

"She's stable, vitals good. Still hasn't woken up."

A knock came at the door. Debra, the front desk receptionist, entered the room. "Officer Scott? Your nine a.m. is here."

"Thanks, Deb." Lucas stood and circled the desk as Deb trotted back down the hall. He addressed Brielle. "I think it's best you're not here when he comes in."

"It's okay. I have to call a client anyway."

"Speaking of, did you get your cell phone back? I left it with Deb this morning."

"She gave it to me, thanks." She compressed her lips, regarding him steadily. "Well, I'd better get. I hope the interview goes well."

"Me, too." He shoved his hands in his pockets as he escorted her to the doorway. "Do you mind praying that we get some answers today?"

"Of course." She started into the hallway then suddenly stopped, facing him again. Lucas's jaw tightened as her arms wrapped around him.

"Thank you, Lucas." She spoke into his shoulder. "You're helping us so much by being here."

"I'm glad I can be here." *With you*, he didn't say.

"Hey, group hug time." Jasper's voice rumbled down the hall like a sonic boom. Lucas and Brielle jumped apart. Brielle backed into the hallway as Jasper approached, then she turned and brushed past her brother.

"Is she okay?" Jasper asked a touch too loudly.

"Yes, uh, she was just saying thank-you."

"Huh." Jasper's gaze sharpened on Lucas for several excruciating seconds, then he shrugged. "You ready to talk to Donaldson?"

"Yes." Lucas cleared his throat. "Let's get the interview started." He pointed at Dash. "Do you normally conduct interviews with him in his crate?"

"Absolutely. It keeps the interviewee on their toes. Be right back."

Lucas retreated to the desk and wiped away the sweat beading his temples.

Larger police stations often had interview rooms, but the Tunnel Creek police station wasn't set up that way. Instead, they'd interview Mr. Donaldson in Jasper's office. Jasper had said Lucas could lead the questioning.

One minute later Aidan Donaldson entered the room, and Lucas tried not to stare. He was exceptionally tall and thin, a mop of gray curls topping his narrow face. Thick black glasses and a trimmed mustache accentuated a built-in scowl.

"Mr. Donaldson. Come in." Lucas motioned at the chair Brielle just vacated, then waited for Jasper to bring in a folding chair and place it opposite the Gaineses' estate manager. Which left Mr. Donaldson about three feet from Dash, who was resting but wide awake in his crate.

"I do hope this won't take too long. I just arrived back in town." Mr. Donaldson's British accent curled his words. He peered around the office, his observant, irritated gaze resting on Dash for several seconds. "I need to schedule the appraisal with the Realtor."

Lucas jumped right in. "You're selling the mansion?"

"We are," Mr. Donaldson confirmed. "Mr. Gaines—Ronald—spoke to me about it at length before his death."

"Tell me a little about your relationship with the deceased."

"We are—we were—longtime friends and business associates, and I mediated with his lawyers to write up his will. I'm the executor. As far as the mansion, he had planned on selling it the end of the year, actually."

"Was Mr. Gaines ill?" Lucas asked.

"No." Mr. Donaldson hesitated a touch too long. "Just the normal aging and health issues."

"Such as..." Lucas prompted.

"He had an arrhythmia that had worsened over these past two years. Stress, gaining too much weight." Mr. Donaldson sniffed. "I urged him to lose weight and exercise, even put in that workout room in the basement, but he always preferred his hobbies."

"And what kind of hobbies did Ronald Gaines have?"

"He collected things. Vintage wine. Artwork. Smelly

old books. Those wretched dinosaur bones. Well, that was, until…"

"Until…" Jasper encouraged him. "Did something happen?"

"It's no secret, officer. There were some financial issues when Peter took over the construction business a few years ago. That's taken care of, however, and no longer affects the family. I'm certain you can look it up for yourself. I'll say nothing more about it."

Lucas's gaze flared into Jasper's. They'd found that Gaines Construction defaulted on two loans about a decade ago, and then filed for bankruptcy shortly afterward. He'd contacted a forensic accountant to go over the last few years' worth of bank accounts.

"Moving on." Lucas clasped his hands and set them on the desk. "We have a few questions for you. As you likely know, a man came after Brielle Holt in her place of business two mornings ago. The day after she heard Peter and Stella arguing in their deceased father's bedroom. Do you know about that incident?"

"I do."

"Where were you that day?"

"I already told you. My niece, Isabella, was getting married. I flew to New Jersey. It was a preset family matter that I couldn't cancel."

"Despite your longtime employer dying a few days before," Jasper muttered.

Mr. Donaldson reared his head toward Jasper. "Yes, despite that. My family is important to me, Officer…?"

"Officer Holt. As is mine." Jasper glared back at the older man.

"Mr. Donaldson…" Lucas interrupted the staring contest. "Jasper," he warned. "Moving on. So you spoke with

Ms. Holt the afternoon of the argument in the Gaineses' residence? You told her it was alright to go back?"

"Yes."

"You told her, I quote, 'Give them some space, and try again.'" Lucas rubbed his chin in an exaggerated gesture, pinning Mr. Donaldson with an expectant look. "Why wouldn't you just tell her it was a bad time? The family is still mourning, et cetera, and have her come back another day?"

"Because Mr. Gaines, Ronald, designated in his will that he wanted his house sold and the contents of the home sold and split between his two children. And my job was to oversee it. If he were still alive, he could corroborate all of this. But his will speaks for itself."

"But he's not alive."

"No, he's not," Mr. Donaldson ground out. "Clearly. But life doesn't stop with death. We all know that. Now, what is the purpose of all these questions if you're just asking what you already know?"

"Mr. Donaldson, do you know Theodore Hardwick?"

Lucas watched the older man's expression. His bristly brows knotted up, and his watery eyes swerved over Lucas's face. Pondering, then confusion.

"I do not. I've never heard of this man."

"You sure about that?" Jasper asked with steel in his words. "Because he attacked Shonda Barkley and my sister. At least twice. Possibly three times. We're pretty certain that's the man who went after her at the Gaineses' mansion yesterday."

"*Pretty certain* doesn't cut it in police work, now does it?"

"What are you and Peter Gaines hiding?" Jasper stood with a growl. Dash did the same, his sleek form slipping halfway out of the crate.

"Jasper," Lucas warned.

Jasper blew out a hard breath and spoke to Dash. The dog lay back down but didn't rest his head on his paws. Instead, he trained his intimidating gaze on Mr. Donaldson.

"Is that dog going to bite me?"

"Not if you tell the truth."

Lucas almost rolled his eyes. "Moving on. As Officer Holt mentioned, a man came after Brielle Holt at the mansion yesterday. Which means someone let him in the house." He stared pointedly at Mr. Donaldson.

"Not necessarily. The mansion is situated adjacent to a national forest. He could've followed her up there and broken into the house. We've all heard about the Backyard Bandit. I believe that's who you should be after."

"We are after him. We're *this* close to catching him—" Lucas pinched his pointer finger and thumb close together. "So you didn't know someone was living in the basement of the Gaineses' mansion?"

"I did not."

"And did you know the purse stolen from Ms. Holt at Long's Lumber was found down there as well?"

Mr. Donaldson appeared momentarily confused, then brushed it off. "I did not."

"What about Peter?" Jasper interjected. "He claims the same thing. Yet, how could you both not know someone was down there?"

Mr. Donaldson sighed loudly. "I stay part-time in the apartment above the garage. It's where I work when I'm here, as well. Rarely do I go down in the basement." Then he looked back at Lucas. "But I do not believe Peter or Stella would instigate something such as this."

"Tell me about their relationship."

"Do you have siblings, Agent Scott?"

"I do not."

"Well, the connection between siblings is always a complicated one."

"That's true," Jasper conceded. "It sounds like Peter and Stella Gaineses' relationship was more than complicated. It sounds like their disagreement over their father's money may have turned deadly."

"Please, Officer Holt, Stella Gaines weighs ninety-eight pounds soaking wet and didn't survive long in Hollywood because she suffers from poor health and chronic migraines. And Peter Gaines hired a bodyguard when he was going through bankruptcy after receiving a threat from a former customer ten years older than I. Peter is terrified of his own shadow."

"Understood." Lucas held still. "Continue, please."

"Stella and Peter have never been close. There have been...arguments and issues between them for many years. I try to keep the peace as best I can."

"So you don't think either of them are hiding a secret from the other." Lucas gazed into Aidan Donaldson's hooded gray eyes. Three heartbeats into the stare down, the older man looked away.

"That is all I have to say about this matter without my lawyer." Mr. Donaldson inhaled and drew up straight.

"Well, that's it then." Lucas cocked his head. "I would like to let you know we're obtaining a warrant to search the entire premises."

"What on earth will that accomplish? Just upset Stella more? And Peter. He's not going to take kindly to this intrusion, especially right after his father's death. He's already furious about us selling the items."

"You believe they're both innocent, and they're not connected to the man who attacked Ms. Barkley and Ms. Holt and was living in Mr. Gaines's house. On a mattress in the basement. That's where Ms. Holt uncovered her purse from a previous attack."

Mr. Donaldson shrugged nonchalantly. "A homeless thief has taken up residence in the mansion. This, this Backyard Bandit, right? Perhaps he stole the purse and broke into the Gaineses' basement recently. Everyone in a thirty-mile radius of this backwoods little town heard that Ronald Gaines died."

Lucas pressed his elbows to the desk and settled his gaze deep into Aidan Donaldson's. "Just know, if there is a connection between one of you and Theodore Hardwick, we will find it. And there will be arrests."

"Am I done?"

"We're done."

After Jasper saw Mr. Donaldson out the door, Lucas rammed a hand through his hair. The estate manager was withholding information. He was sure of it. But what information—and *why*?

NINE

Brielle closed the gardening magazine as Lucas entered the station break room. She tried not to stare as he sat next to her on the worn leather couch. His profile, the strong nose, sand-colored, short-cropped hair, and strong jaw all drew her attention, and his glasses added a studious air that fit him and his intelligence.

"How'd it go?" she asked.

"Wasn't bad. Wasn't good, either. We're working on securing a warrant to search the mansion."

"Brielle. Lucas," Jasper interrupted, popping into the break room, an adult version of his wiggly son. "Kinsley's water broke. She's in labor. I'm heading to the hospital." Then he disappeared.

"Jasper!" Brielle called out. She and Lucas rose and hurried after him. "What can we do to help?"

"Can you guys follow me? Mom's bringing Gabe, too, but they might not stay. No good having a kid in the hospital too long. Lucas, can you follow up on the warrant? Check in with Judge DeMarco. Make sure she knows we need this warrant ASAP. The medical examiner should be back in town soon, and I expect her call any minute."

"You got it," Lucas answered.

"Oh," Jasper continued, "I need someone to take Dash

back to the cabin. Make sure the dogs get fed and taken outside—"

"Hey." Lucas set his hand on Jasper's shoulder. "We got it covered. We'll take Dash back to the cabin and take care of the dogs. We can grab anything Kinsley forgot or needs."

"Right, good. Thanks." Jasper blinked past Brielle. "That's good."

"Want me to pray for her and the baby?" Lucas asked.

Jasper's posture loosened. "Yeah, man. I'd sure appreciate that."

Lucas bowed his head as they stood in the break room, with phones ringing down the hall and officers trekking back and forth, Dash sitting at Jasper's heel and Brielle's heart suddenly three sizes larger in her chest. The baby was coming!

Lucas said, "Amen," and she and Jasper echoed it.

"Thanks, man."

They made their way outside to the vehicles, and Jasper loaded Dash into the back of the white, unmarked Charger Lucas and she were driving, clipping the dog's leash into the seat belt and crooning to his partner. Then he took off for his vehicle.

"Jasper, wait." She jogged after her big brother, wrapping him in a tight embrace that she needed as much as he did. This big, teasing lug of a man who was an expert at protecting and provoking her. "I love you."

"Love you, too." He pulled back and looked down at her with worried brown eyes.

"God will be watching over Kinsley and baby girl."

He cocked his head and smiled. "It's really nice to hear you say that." He tweaked her arm, then headed for his car. Brielle pivoted and climbed in beside Luas. Dash let out a whine from the back seat when Jasper drove away.

"You'll see him soon," she said to her brother's loyal

K9 partner. When she glanced at Lucas, she found him watching her, his expression thoughtful and almost proud. “What?”

He started up the car. “You should’ve seen Jasper’s face when you hugged him. I don’t know what you said, but whatever it was, it helped him.”

“I told him I loved him. And that God would watch over Kinsley and the baby.”

“That’s a great reminder before a major life event.”

“He’s my brother. I do love him.” She swallowed. “I know I’ve let them down by staying away too much.”

He steered the car out onto the main road, heading east toward Jasper’s cabin. They passed the Tunnel Creek Drive-In and Marvin’s Diner, and Lucas’s amiable, patient silence prompted her to share more.

“I used to help my dad at the school where they taught in Cameroon. Dad taught English and PE, and Mom taught art. The people in our village were so grateful, and the kids so sweet and friendly.” She twined her fingers together on her lap. “I loved helping Dad teach the younger kids how to read. I helped mom with her art stuff, but sometimes it felt like I didn’t do the projects right. Plus all the mess.”

“You were a daddy’s girl.”

“I guess you could say that.” How was it possible to smile and frown at the same time?

“Do you ever wonder what your life would’ve been like if…”

“If my dad was still alive?” She wadded up air in her cheeks then released it. “Yes, sometimes. But he’s been gone so long, it’s hard to imagine that now.”

“The day before Leah died, we had a big fight.” Lucas adjusted his grip on the steering wheel, staring straight ahead as he spoke.

"I'm sorry, that must've made everything that much more painful."

"Yes, for sure it did."

They entered the forest, and the sunlight faded as trees overshadowed the road.

"Do you mind me asking what you fought about?" Was she being too nosy?

He didn't answer for several seconds. "I thought…we had our relationship timeline all worked out. Leah and I were engaged, and we'd planned on waiting until the summer after college graduation to get married. I felt that was the more responsible route, since we'd both have jobs at that point. She with teaching, and me on the police force."

"That sounds reasonable."

"I thought so, too. But a couple of weeks before Leah died, she changed her mind. Really wanted to get married. Fast. It came out of left field, and I was taken aback. She pressured me, so much so that I questioned…us."

"That's a tough situation," she said quietly.

"But there was something about Leah that no one, not even I, knew."

Her breath caught in her lungs as she waited for him to elaborate.

"We didn't live perfect lives, and…after she was killed, the coroner told her parents her secret. Leah was nine weeks pregnant. Suddenly I understood why she wanted to get married so quickly."

"Oh, Lucas…" She released the breath in a harsh exhale. "I'm so sorry. That must've been like two deaths."

"Yeah, it was. What a terrible fiancé I was for not knowing what was going on with her, and not asking what caused her change of heart about waiting to get married."

"You didn't know. Her parents…?"

"Still won't talk to me." His posture slumped in the seat.

"They didn't blame me for her death, per se, but knowing what transpired, and understanding that Leah was upset with me, they believe that caused their daughter to make the poor decisions she did that night."

"What do you mean? I thought..." Brielle frowned. Her understanding was that Leah was visiting someone near Greenville the weekend she died.

"Leah had a childhood friend who lived near Greenville. Reagan was a partier, and I'd never been a fan of Leah hanging out with her. Leah knew going there would bother me. So she drove out to see Reagan that weekend. I'd been upset with her, telling her I wasn't ready to get married and reminding her of our plan."

She swallowed, hating that the end to this story was a tragic one.

"So she met Reagan at a local bar that night. She even called me from the bar, but I was still annoyed and didn't answer. Then when I called her back two hours later, near midnight, she didn't answer." He swiped at his eyes. "The man had followed her and...she was already gone."

Brielle reached over and settled her left hand over his right one as he drove up Jasper and Kinsley's driveway. She wasn't sure what to say, so she didn't say anything.

"Thanks for listening." He squeezed her hand once, twice, then pulled away. "That's why it's hard to come back. There are reminders all over this town. Reminders of how I failed her." He parked the car and they climbed out before she could refute his statement. "Do you mind if I make a quick call? I need to contact the judge one more time and try to nail down this warrant for the Gaineses' place."

"Sure. I'll be inside." Brielle walked into the house beside Dash. She greeted the other three dogs, fed them, and let them run around out back. Then she brought Leo, Mike, Dash, and Trek back inside and freshened their water. A cloud hung over her after her conversation with Lucas. He believed he was at least partially responsible for Leah's death.

No wonder he doesn't like visiting. He would never consider staying here.

Over the last few days, she'd gotten to know Lucas Scott even better. He'd proven he was still the same thoughtful, intelligent, and kind person he'd been in high school. Lucas made her think and laugh, and he enjoyed talking about books. He was a man of character, one who was trustworthy and dependable—despite the fact he believed he had something to do with Leah's untimely, tragic death.

A melancholy smile played with her lips. Too bad Lucas only viewed her as Jasper's sister. Only cared about her as a friend.

Lucas had made that clear. And once this scary investigation was over, the case solved, he had no interest in staying in Tunnel Creek.

Lucas hung up with Judge DeMarco's assistant, then strode into the Holt's cabin. The warrant would be issued tomorrow sometime, the man had promised.

"Brielle?" He looked around for her. Their conversation in the car still lingered in his thoughts. He hadn't even shared those details with his parents, after Leah's death. Surely, Brielle would think less of him now that he'd admitted his and Leah's mistakes, and his role in her death.

One of his biggest regrets about Leah was that she probably felt abandoned. And he'd spent the better part of a decade trying to make sure no one else on his watch felt that way again.

Not that he could stop crime. Of course, he couldn't. But when family members wanted justice—wanted to know their loved one didn't die in vain—that gave him the drive to comb through the scene and evidence to find the criminal. Get them off the street.

"I'm up here," she called from the second floor.

Lucas took the stairs two at a time and followed the noise of a thousand dog claws on wood floors. Brielle rifled through a dresser in Jasper and Kinsley's bedroom, all four dogs in various spots around the room. She held a small duffel bag.

"Jasper texted and asked for socks and extra clothes for her. Also, Gabe's Transformers for the waiting room. Would you mind grabbing a couple from his bedroom?"

Transformers? He had this covered. "Which ones does he want?"

"You were an eight-year-old boy once. You decide." She grinned, and his stomach muscles tightened. He tugged his gaze from her and tapped the doorframe on his way down the hall.

It was so good to see her smiling and teasing him and her brothers again, despite what had happened this week. But that smile. *Her smile.* It made him consider things he shouldn't be considering.

How could he imagine letting himself care for someone again? No, *love* someone. Brielle deserved no less than his whole heart, and he had a sinking feeling it would be incredibly easy to hand it over to her. But that would mean staying here in Tunnel Creek, where memories taunted him, weighed him down.

Not the place where he'd failed Leah.

He shook it all off as he entered Gabe's room. Wallpapered in Transformer posters and boasting shelves stocked with half-finished Lego sets, the room screamed *boy.* Lucas crouched to search a baseball-shaped toy bin. He grabbed three toys, then stood. His phone buzzed in his pocket.

Chief McCoy. "Lucas Scott here."

"Lucas. Matt Reed just clocked a driver going eighty out on state road sixty-four. He followed the guy. The tags come back, guess who, Theodore Hardwick. The truck got pretty far ahead, turned up a country road and by the time Matt reached the vehicle, it was empty."

Lucas squeezed the plastic toys in his grasp until his palms hurt. "No sign of the driver?"

"None so far. I called Jasper but he's at the hospital. Bad timing. Listen, the man is in the forest between sixty-four and the Broken Branch River. Not many places to hide. Sure wish we could use Dash to ferret him out. It'd need to be soon. Like, ASAP."

"I'm not sure how Dash will do with me, but I'm willing to try."

Tunnel Creek PD was a small force, and Dash was the only active K9 officer on duty.

"Might be smart to get another one trained and in the office," McCoy acknowledged. "Meantime, you mind calling Jasper and finding out if he thinks Dash will work with you or another officer? We need to track this guy down."

Yes, they did. Lucas hung up with McCoy and called Jasper. Brielle appeared in the doorway, questions in her eyes. He reached out a hand, offering her the toys he'd chosen. She took them just as Jasper answered the call.

"I'm sorry to bother you. Kinsley and baby doing okay?"

"They're good. Baby isn't here yet. Kinsley is doing amazing. Man, I'm glad I'm not a woman."

"And we are, too." Lucas cleared his throat and grinned as Brielle made a funny face. "I assume you talked to McCoy and you know what's happening?"

"I do and I did. I can see how things progress, then head out to sixty-four—"

"Absolutely not. I'll go. I just need to know if Dash will work with me."

"He should. He worked with Matt Reed for a drug bust when I was on medical leave. I just..." Jasper let off, and Lucas waited. Jasper loved that dog like his own flesh and blood.

"I'll be careful. I won't risk injury to Dash, I promise."

"Thanks, man. I'd appreciate it. Kinsley's strong and she's doing good, but it would kill me to leave now."

Leah's face came to mind, and he closed his eyes. "I wouldn't want to, either."

They finished discussing the details about how to prepare Dash for the field, and then Jasper mentioned Brielle. "Can you drop off Brielle on your way?"

"Absolutely. She'll be safe there with you." He met her eyes. She nodded at him.

"Right. Thanks, man. I appreciate this."

Lucas said goodbye then hung up.

"Are you sure you should do this?" she asked.

"I want this man caught. You and Shonda deserve that." Poor Shonda. While her condition remained stable and the doctors were optimistic, she still hadn't woken up.

They packed up the items and loaded Dash's bulletproof K9 vest and leash, plus his stuffed squirrel Rocky into the Charger. Moments later they were back on the road, headed into Tunnel Creek. The hospital was only a mile from the police station. Lucas's mind filed through what he'd seen Jasper do with Dash. How they went after criminals on foot. It would be nearly an hour from the time the suspect ran to when he and Dash would get there, so it wasn't likely they would catch him at this point.

He clenched his jaw. They had to try.

"I'm worried about you and Dash going alone," Brielle said, as they pulled to a four-way stop.

"There will be another officer. We need to catch him.

Think about it. You've lost your freedom to work. To drive around. To live."

She nodded solemnly.

A question came to mind as he drove through the intersection. "Will Noah and his fiancée be at the hospital?"

"I think so. Noah works three twelves, and he just finished that shift yesterday, Mom said. So hopefully he and Lucy can make it to meet baby."

"So, they know it's a girl but haven't decided on a name?"

"They've decided but didn't want to share it yet."

"What would you do? If it was you? Would you have a name chosen yet?"

She tilted her head. "I think I would want to know his or her name. To call them that. What about you?"

"I'd need a name because I'd be discussing the best chapter books for our, I mean, for my son or daughter to read in fifth grade."

Brielle giggled.

She must not have heard his slipup. To even consider the idea he was worthy of having a child of his own after what he'd allowed to happen to Leah. No. Those thoughts weren't even worth entertaining.

They passed the police station, then Tunnel Creek General Hospital came into view. The white and gray three-story building stood out among the humble brick-and-glass storefronts along the main road in town.

Lucas pulled up at the front doors. His gaze traveled over the parking lot and the people entering the hospital. "I don't want to leave Dash. I'll stay here and wait for your text that you made it safely to the waiting room and your family."

"Please be safe out there." She reached back to scratch Dash's ears, then looked intently at Lucas. "Both of you."

"We will."

"Thank you for doing this for Jasper."

"I'm doing this for you, too, Brielle. You've been through so much already." He hesitated. "I can't stand the thought of something else happening to you."

Before he could react, she leaned across the console and cupped his cheek. Then she turned, exited the car, and hurried into the hospital double doors. He sat there, the heat gathered on his face, waiting for her text. Trying not to read too much into her tender parting touch.

Finally his phone pinged.

I'm in the waiting room with my mom. Be safe.

I will. I'll pray the baby gets here soon and safely.

And I'll pray you come back here soon and safely.

Lucas read and reread the last text. She said she'd pray for him twice today. *Lord, help her faith in You grow even stronger.*

No, he told his heart. Don't even think it.

Right now, the only thing he could let his mind focus on was catching Theodore Hardwick. Getting Brielle out of harm's way so she could return to the life and job she loved.

Once this case was solved, he'd head back to Myrtle Beach and a life that might be a little lonely but was fulfilling and kept the guilt and regret at bay. And that was enough.

TEN

Brielle sat across from her middle brother, Noah, and his fiancée, Lucy, in the hospital waiting room. Gabe was squished in between them, showing Lucy how to unfold one of the Transformer toys Lucas had chosen. Lucy was a social worker with the state, championing children in difficult situations. She'd also been a sweet friend in high school. Noah had struck gold with her. And the way they looked at each other…

She averted her gaze. Seeing the unspoken communication and connection made her think of Lucas. Between the baby's imminent arrival and Lucas out in the woods with Dash, chasing the man who'd come after her, her thoughts were awhirl.

Brielle offered another prayer for his safety, then looked at her mom, who sat in the chair opposite Brielle. Mom's brown hair was streaked with gray and caught in a messy braid, and her different-colored nails tapped away on a text on her phone. Probably to her prayer group from church about Kinsley.

Mom had always been creative, full of ideas and energy. An artist through and through.

And faith. Brielle still remembered waking up and finding her mom at the foot of her bed. Praying. She sank lower in the hard plastic seat. There had been times she hadn't believed those prayers made a difference.

Hadn't even wanted them. *Forgive me, Lord.*

And that seemed to make her mom all the more determined to pray. Sometime in her preteen years—probably a couple years after Dad's death and their move back to the states—Brielle had allowed her grief to turn into anger. And that anger had formed a wall between her and God, a wall that had felt impenetrable and unbreakable for all of her adult life.

Please, Lord. Forgive me. I'm sorry for my anger. I don't want to waste any more of my life with distance between me and You, Lord, or between me and my family.

"I'm so nervous." Mom wore a bashful grin. "I can't believe we get to hold baby girl soon. Finally. At least her room is done."

Her mom had painted a colorful forest and field mural on the nursery wall, with birds in the air and animals on the green grass.

"It's beautiful," Lucy said. "She'll be growing up in the woods inside the cabin and out."

"Yes, Mom, it looks great." Noah echoed, twining Lucy's hand with his. He glanced at Lucy, then at Brielle. "I think we're going to go for a walk downstairs. What do you say, Gabe? You want to go stretch your legs and grab something to eat?" Noah chuckled as Gabe pushed his toothpick legs out, then he looked at Brielle and their mom. "You all need anything?"

"I'm fine, thank you, hon." Mom slipped her cell in her purse.

"I'm good, thanks." Brielle watched as they filed out of the waiting room, their hands still linked, Gabe clinging to Lucy's arm.

"I can hardly wait to find out what baby girl's name is.

I can't believe they tortured us by not telling us until now." Mom teasingly proclaimed.

"On the way over here, Lucas and I agreed that we would've shared the name by now."

Her mom chuckled. "I'm with you on that. I wouldn't be able to keep my mouth shut." Her eyes glazed over with memories. "Your dad could hardly wait to meet you three, either. He was so, so nervous with Jasper. Handled him like he was fine China. Then, with Noah he was just as excited, but held him like he was a football while chasing after Jasper."

Brielle pictured her dad, dark hair and mustache, teaching students to read and how to throw a football. Imagining him holding one baby and chasing a toddler was difficult, especially since the thought of either of her strapping brothers as babies or toddlers was almost comical.

"When your dad and I found out you were a girl, he was beside himself. And when you arrived? That silly man acted like you were made of glass." She chortled, then her expression turned pensive. "He loved you all equally, but you were your daddy's little girl. Prayed for and well-loved. He was so happy to have you in our family."

Happy. A wellspring of memories and emotions collided, making her eyes sting. "It feels so long ago that I saw him last," Brielle whispered. "Like a dream almost."

"Yes, and I've missed him every day." Mom paused. "I know that you blame me." Her words were as fragile as a dried flower bouquet.

"Mom, I don't, really..." She swallowed, peering around the nearly empty waiting room. "I was a child when it happened. I realize now, kids tend to have skewed memories of events."

"That might be the case, but *I* realize now that I should've gotten us all into counseling after we returned stateside."

Brielle's chest tightened. "Do you think I'm messed up because of Dad's death?"

Her mom rose to her feet and came over, kneeling in front of Brielle. "No, hon. Not at all. I don't mean that. I just wonder if that might've helped us work through some of the issues that come with losing a parent so young. Issues that came between us. I'm sorry I didn't do that."

Brielle drew in a fortifying breath. "I know Dad told you to stay behind. With…me."

"Ah. So, you overheard that."

Brielle nodded, her chin quivering.

"It's true, hon. He did say that. Wait a minute, have you blamed *yourself* for his death?" Her mom's voice was incredulous.

Brielle could only nod as her throat closed around a swell of emotion.

"Oh, Brielle. No, no. It wasn't… There's something else you three don't know." Tears flooded Mom's lower lashes, and Brielle helped her rise and drop into the seat beside her. She wrapped an arm around Mom's shoulders and let her take her time with whatever she needed to say next.

"I wasn't truthful with you, hon. Not…really."

"What do you mean?"

"Your dad didn't get *lost*, Brielle." Mom opened her mouth, inhaled slowly, then exhaled. Finally, she turned to Brielle. "One of the men from our village found your dad, that much was true. But he didn't die lost in the wild. I told you that because I didn't want you children scared. The truth is, a group of…unruly men…followed him out of Douala and took the medical supplies and money he had on him." She closed her eyes. "Then they shot him."

Brielle held still as her mom's words came to life in her mind. "He wasn't lost?"

"No. And if I *hadn't* stayed behind, you and your brothers very likely would've lost both your parents." She twined her arm with Brielle's and sank her head on her shoulder. "Can you forgive me for keeping that from you all these years?"

"Yes, Mom, I forgive you." She squeezed her mom's hand, her chest somehow light and heavy at the same time. What a terrible situation for Mom to deal with, all while she was serving the Lord. It was hard to believe her mom wasn't much older at that time than Brielle was now. "But how did you survive his loss? And not get mad at God?"

"I did get mad at God! We'd gone overseas to serve Him and those in need, and look what happened. Anger and I were good friends for a long while. But God reminded me that I had you three to care for still. Blessed little living breathing pieces of me and of your wonderful, sweet father. My life wasn't over. I wasn't the only woman who lost her husband young, you know? That helped me stay focused on what was important. Which was—still is—you and your brothers."

Jasper burst into the waiting room. "Baby girl is here!" A frown rode his brow as he noticed them huddled together. "Are you okay, Mom?"

She and Mom stood as one unit. Separate—but together. *For where your treasure is, there will your heart be also.*

"Yes, I am most definitely okay. Brielle, how about you?" Brielle nodded, beaming. Mom addressed Jasper. "How is Kinsley?"

"Good." He grinned. "They're weighing and measuring her. Man, she's beautiful. They both are. Any news from Lucas?"

Brielle checked her phone. "Not so far."

He gave a quick nod. "I'll come down when it's clear for you to see her." Then he disappeared, taking his slaphappy grin with him.

"I'll text Noah." Her mom tapped on her phone.

A few minutes later Jasper returned, motioning them to follow. Brielle's heart soared as they all entered the delivery room. Kinsley lay on the bed, her long hair pulled back, cheeks shining. A triumphant, weary smile on her face. Brielle's mom beelined for the baby bassinet on the other side of Kinsley's bed.

"Oh, sweetie. Look how beautiful she is." Mom swiped at tears, then cradled the softly mewling baby to her chest. Brielle and Lucy approached the little pink bundle of new life and tears fell down her cheeks, too. Brielle had been working in Greenville when Gabe was born and hadn't seen him until he was a month old.

Regret and sadness circled her throat, growing into a sob she barely held back. She should've been there for Gabe's birth, too. Should've come to support Jasper, especially since his marriage to his ex-wife had been troubled from the start.

Her mom turned to face Kinsley. "Please, for the love of acrylic paint and canvas, what is this little sweet pea's name?"

Jasper's gaze crashed into Kinsley's. A silent but clear communication happened, filled with love and joy and trust.

"Her name is Margaret Dana Holt," Jasper answered reverentially. "We're calling her Maggie."

Brielle's chest constricted, and a sudden longing took her breath away at the deep affection between Jasper and Kinsley. It was a palpable force in the room. Lucas's face swam through her watery vision. His serious expressions and steady presence. His grace and understanding about her distance from her family. His rare, handsome grin and the shocking blue of his eyes.

No. She had to stop this, whatever *this* was. Her high

school crush, returning full force and at an inopportune time. He would head home when the case was solved. And she couldn't leave Tunnel Creek. Or her family. Not now that she and her mom had laid bare their misunderstandings and the pain of the past.

She blinked away her tears and spent the next few minutes cooing over sweet little Maggie alongside her mom, Noah, and Lucy. Even Gabe wanted a turn to hold his new sister. Every couple minutes, she'd check her phone. Nothing from Lucas.

What was happening out there?

Lucas checked Dash's K9 vest once more and made sure the leash was secure. To his left, Officer Matt Reed leaned into his squad car to grab his flashlight. A few feet down the road, stuck in a ditch, sat the dark blue truck that had been near Brielle's store a couple days ago and the same one that had run them down by the sawmill the next day.

"Ready?" Matt asked.

"Yes." They jogged over to the truck, checking the exterior of the vehicle before opening the door and allowing Dash to scent items inside. Lucas joined him. *There it was.* A pungent, woodsy scent. Just like Brielle had said. He was fairly certain that was patchouli oil.

Lucas wrinkled his nose.

Matt asked Dash to sniff the discarded ball cap on the front seat. Food wrappers, plastic bags, and—aha—a pair of expensive shoes shoved under a seat were the only other items. One receipt they confiscated. The bed of the truck held a few dented tools but nothing outstanding that visibly connected the suspect to the crimes. No sign of a cell phone.

They withdrew from the truck, then started toward the field on the ridge past the road. Matt asked Dash to smell the hat again, then encouraged the K9 to seek the suspect.

The agile dog shot up and over the ridge, then took off into the field. Lucas and Matt jogged after him, Lucas on the left, Matt on the right, their utility belts clanking as they ran. Matt called out commands every few seconds, and Dash circled back for them. The dog let out successive, excited yips as he returned to the trail and forged ahead. The afternoon sun was drooping in the sky, leaving behind shadows among the trees and earth still damp from the recent storms.

Three minutes later they came upon a pebble-strewn creek, one that, according to Matt, was a small tributary of the Broken Branch River. McCoy believed the suspect might make it to the Broken Branch then turn around, as the river was deep and not easy to cross. The swath of woods they searched was several square miles, Lucas noted on a map, and there was no way to be sure the suspect was still nearby.

Still, the man could attempt to swim across the Broken Branch. Then Dash might lose the scent.

Matt called out a command when Dash tried to cross the creek. The dog loped through the shallow water then stopped, tongue lolling. Ferns and low bushes edged the creek, and Lucas paced the muddy sides, looking for footprints while catching his breath.

Dash whined, then sat on his haunches.

"He wants to keep going." Matt patted Dash and praised him, then bent forward, chest heaving. "See anything?"

"Not so far. My guess is this perp went north—" Lucas pointed "—and will try to come back around. There's a bunch more woods out there, even past the Broken Branch. He could try to lead us away, then return and drive off."

"Alright, let's keep at it." Matt released Dash, and the dog bounded across the creek and disappeared through the ferns and foliage on the other side.

Lucas leapt the creek, too, not quite as gracefully as Dash. He and Matt jogged after him. A few minutes later, they left the woods and entered a small meadow. Dash plunged on ahead, his lithe frame and swift stride eating up the ground. No wonder Jasper stayed in shape. When Dash neared the reentry to the woods past the meadow, Matt whistled, calling out for the dog to return.

Instead, Dash thundered into the woods, a powerful volley of barking exploding across the treetops.

"He found him!" Matt raced ahead, calling out commands and identifying himself, his weapon drawn. Lucas sprinted after him, tugging out his weapon as they approached. He tapped the shoulder radio and called in their location and the events. Dispatch relayed they had backup coming.

A gunshot exploded through the woods, then another. Vicious growling burned Lucas's ears as he entered the fray.

"Drop your weapon!" Lucas ran up to the writhing pile of criminal and police dog in a muddy clearing. Matt lay off to the side, one hand on his chest. Dash had a secure hold of the suspect's weapon arm, his powerful jaws drawing blood. The man screamed, his gun flailing in the air.

Lucas catalogued the scene in seconds. Matt looked like he'd been shot, but there was no visible blood. Bullet must've struck his vest and knocked the wind out of him. Blood poured down the suspect's arm. Suddenly, the man tugged a knife from his pocket with his other hand, his face contorted in determination. He was going to try to stab Dash.

"Dash, release!" Lucas aimed high rather than at the center mass because that would put the shot too close to Dash. Then he fired a split second before the man's left arm swung in an arc with the knife, right at Dash. The bullet tore through the man's left shoulder, and the knife *thunked* to the ground.

Lucas approached the groaning, bleeding suspect. His heart felt like a wild creature in his chest, and he focused to slow his breathing.

"Dash, easy," he said. The dog circled the man, growling and whining, his muscular body quivering.

"Good boy. Check perimeter. Matt, talk to me." The dog trotted in a widening circle around them as Lucas hurried over to the other officer writhing on the ground. "Matt?"

"I'm okay," Matt mumbled. "Hit my vest. Left side."

"Shots fired," Lucas shouted into his radio. "We need backup here now. Suspect down. I repeat, suspect down. Officer hit but his vest stopped the bullet."

Lucas stood over the prone suspect. An average-looking man, early forties. Brown eyes and hair and acne scars on his sneering face. His straight white teeth caught in a grimace as blood seeped out of the gunshot wound.

"You're getting…nothing…from me."

"We'll see about that." Hatred spewed like hot lava inside Lucas, the dangerous, dark emotion seeping through his veins. His nostrils flared as he gripped his gun and stared at the man who'd attacked Brielle multiple times and nearly killed her coworker. His finger flickered over the trigger.

Greater is he who is in you, than he who is in the world.

The verse split the hatred, broke apart the rage, and finally subdued the lethal thoughts circling his mind.

If the suspect lived, he would be charged with the crimes he committed. Attempted murder. Breaking and entering. Resisting arrest. Shooting an officer. And maybe then they'd finally find out if Theodore Hardwick had a connection to the Gaines family.

But for now, Lucas focused on Officer Reed and Dash, and thanked God they were all okay.

ELEVEN

Lucas followed the group of medical personnel through the emergency room doors at Tunnel Creek General. Matt Reed lay on the stretcher, his Kevlar vest removed and an ice pack wrapped around his bare abdomen. Lucas edged out of the hallway as physicians circled Matt and barked out questions, finally taking him back to run tests.

One of them asked if Lucas was okay, but he waved them off.

Their pursuit of the suspect had covered a lot of ground, and exhaustion plus spent adrenaline made him feel sluggish and wired at the same time. All told, they must've run two or three miles.

Thank the Lord Matt was okay and the suspect had fired with a handgun and not something deadlier. The Kevlar vest distributed the bullet's impact but still caused a whopper of a bruise underneath, or possibly cracked some ribs. A young woman in her early thirties rushed through the ER doors, her face contorted with worry as she asked around about Matt Reed.

Lucas strode toward her. "Are you Matt's wife?"

"Yes. I'm Lori. Please tell me he's okay. Please. I heard an officer was shot and I got here as quickly as I could."

He gently held her upper arms to get her to focus on him. "Lori, he's okay. He was shot, but his vest saved him.

He's right down there." Lucas pointed out which way to go, and as she hurried through the double doors, his attention snagged on someone else rushing through the lobby doors from the elevator bank.

"Brielle?"

She ran into his arms, worry, relief, and gratitude mapped on her face, and Lucas caught her against him. He closed his eyes as she pressed her face to his neck.

"You're okay." She pulled back to look at him, her gaze sweeping up and down.

"I'm overdue for a nap."

"And Matt? Dash?"

"They're both fine. Matt has a big bruise on his midsection. They're going to run some tests to make sure there are no broken ribs or internal bleeding, but he's likely just going to be sore for a few days. Dash was taken by another officer to the station, where he'll get water, treats, and time in his crate until we pick him up." He cocked his head. "Did the baby arrive?"

"Margaret Dana Holt is here. Maggie. She's…perfect."

"Kinsley's doing alright?"

"She's tired. I think we're all going to head out so she can rest. She'll be leaving tomorrow. The baby's bilirubin level was a little high, so they'll stay tonight and leave tomorrow, Lord willing."

"Lord willing?" Lucas cocked a brow and smiled.

"What? Yes, Lord willing." She smiled hesitantly back. "Come on, you need to meet Maggie before visiting hours are over."

They entered the elevator, and moments later they exited the third floor and treaded slowly down the hall. Inside the dimmed room, Kinsley rested on the bed, while Jasper sprawled next to her in the chair he must've pulled across the room. On the other side of the hospital room,

Dana Holt ambled back and forth, a small white bundle held fast in her arms.

She turned to face him and Brielle when they entered. Lucas gave a quick wave and thumbs-up, then motioned at the new parents. Dana's face curved in a loving smile. Brielle tiptoed over to her, folding her mom in a gentle half hug. They both stared down at the baby, then she whispered something to her mom. Dana nodded, then Brielle pressed a kiss to Dana's cheek.

Lucas crossed the room, his chest warming and the day's stressful events forgotten as he peered down at the tiny, squishy-cheeked newborn. Such a little miracle. A pang of longing tightened his throat, and his gaze flickered into Brielle's. They shared a wonder-filled look and he considered the tender physical gestures between Brielle and her mom.

Had things shifted positively between them?

Brielle and Lucas tiptoed back across the room and headed into the hall.

"Where's Gabe?" he whispered.

"Noah and Lucy took him home. They'll spend the night with him and the dogs at the cabin."

"Good deal." Lucas quietly closed the door, then strolled beside Brielle to the elevator. Once the elevator door closed, Lucas pulled out his phone and checked texts.

"Here we go." He reread the text from Judge DeMarcos. "Excellent. The judge answered our request. She said the warrant will be available midday tomorrow."

Brielle leaned against the shiny metal wall of the elevator. "So it's safe for me to take Gabe to the fair tomorrow?"

"Hold up. I don't know about that."

"You just caught the suspect."

"True, but I can't guarantee Aidan Donaldson and Peter or Stella Gaines aren't involved with this. Something is going on with that family. Speaking of." He checked his phone again. "Mr. Donaldson hasn't returned my texts. Hmm." Maybe the interview had rattled him. Or maybe he refused to answer any more questions until his lawyer was involved.

Lucas rubbed a hand down his face. "Do you really need to go to the fair?"

"I don't want to break my promise to Gabe."

He slid her a sideways look. The resolute expression on her face warned this would be a fight. "I get it. I just don't want you there by yourself."

"I canceled my booth, so I won't be working. But I'd like to make it a fun day for Gabe. Even just for a couple of hours. He's been an only child for so long, and this new baby will be an adjustment. I also think it might help if he's gone tomorrow for a bit when Jasper and Kinsley get home. That'll give them time to themselves."

"We'll have to see." Lucas led Brielle outside, one hand on the small of her back. His attention transferred to their surroundings. The white, unmarked Charger waited on the far side of the lot, sitting alone under a parking lot light. He slowed, eyeing the area, one hand resting on his weapon. She noted the motion and frowned.

"Lucas?"

"Just being cautious."

He led her to the passenger-side door and opened it. Once she was inside, he jogged around the car and folded inside. The evening air had cooled, and gray clouds bunched together on the darkening horizon. The storms were different in Tunnel Creek than in Myrtle Beach. Here they moved in slowly, crawling over the mountains with lots of rumbling and growling, as though angry that the trees slowed them down. Tunnel Creek felt more sheltered than Myrtle Beach, nearer to the Atlantic, where pop-up lightning-heavy thunderheads were a way of life.

He took a left toward his parents' condo, his mind moving backward to the book he still needed to give her. He was surprised she hadn't mentioned it yet.

Speaking of books. "So, the garden scene."

Brielle giggled. "This *again*?"

"I'm just trying to understand the appeal. You know, look at it from all angles."

"Like a good detective. Right," she teased. "I don't think every person who reads *Jane Eyre* feels this way, Lucas. I simply love the emotions in the scene. They're so raw and real. What scene from a book stayed with you or moved you?"

"Hands down, the scene in *The Martian* where Mark Watney is reunited with the Ares 3 crew."

"Did you cry?"

Lucas scoffed. "I only cry when I'm chopping onions."

"Aw, you *did* cry."

"I never said that." He couldn't help grinning at her. "I specifically said only if I chop onions."

Brielle returned his smile, and in the fading daylight, with streaks of sunset breaking through the car window and the possibility of solving this case in sight, he wondered what life would be like once he couldn't see that smile every day.

He shook off the unwelcome reality check and focused on driving. Brielle likely wouldn't welcome him ruining their friendship by sharing his growing feelings toward her, and Jasper certainly wouldn't approve of them together. Would he?

Leave it alone, Scott.

They were only a mile from his parents' place. A four-way stop lay ahead, then a winding section of road led them to the condo community.

As he approached the intersection, Lucas pressed the brakes. Instead of catching, the pedal felt spongy underfoot. He pumped the brake again. What in the world? The vehicle didn't respond, confirming his fear and matching his racing pulse to their increasing speed.

Someone must've tampered with the brakes. But where—at the hospital or at the mansion? He hit the lights and siren and glanced at the radio on the dash. No time to call anyone now. They were going to fly through the intersection at forty-five miles per hour. Lord willing, no one else was crossing at that time.

"Lucas?"

"The brakes are out. Hang on!"

Brielle clutched the armrest as Lucas began zigzagging the steering wheel, like he was skiing.

"What did you say?" The stop sign warned them of the possibility of oncoming traffic, but Lucas didn't slow down the car.

"The brakes aren't working." He repeated in a whip-tight voice. "This provides friction and slows the vehicle."

"What? Lucas, there's a van up there! On the left."

She barely bottled up a scream as they plowed through the intersection. A car honked to their left, and the screech of brakes burned her ears. The van narrowly missed plowing into Lucas's side of the car.

Thank the Lord the car hadn't hit them. She gaped at the road ahead. The woods pressed against the left side of the road, and an incline on the right was littered with rocks and low bushes and smaller trees. In the darkness, it was tough to see how steeply the ground dropped off on the right. But she knew it was dangerous. How far was the drop? Ten, twenty feet?

Up ahead, a turn in the road loomed. "Is there an emergency brake?"

"The parking brake might lock the back tires. Too risky." He pumped the brakes again, but it didn't decelerate the car. "Hang on."

They approached the turn too fast, and a tingling feeling poured through Brielle's limbs at the awful sensation of not slowing down. The woods blurred, and she gritted her teeth as Lucas fought the momentum of the vehicle. She slammed up against the passenger-side door as they turned to the left, and the tires squealed in protest at the fast, jerky turn.

Please, God, protect us.

The vehicle felt as though it were lifting slightly on the left side. Brielle closed her eyes and tried not to scream at the sharpest portion of the turn. Suddenly, they were on the other side of the curve, and Lucas righted the car with a jarring bounce back to the right. Then he continued to zigzag slightly, back and forth, until her stomach rose into her throat.

"Trying…to add…friction to slow this down."

Two headlights shone up ahead in the dying sunlight, cutting through the woods. Lucas stopped zigzagging and lowered his head, focusing as the car approached in the oncoming lane and blared the horn. The driver must've noticed their speed and erratic driving.

Once the car passed, Brielle released a heavy breath. "There's a small pond up on the right before the condo community."

"A pond?"

"It's not deep. I'm going to run us into that."

"We're driving into a pond?" She clutched the armrest on her right and the console on her left. *Lord, help us slow down.*

Water glimmered up ahead, but it was on the left side, not the right. They'd have to cross into oncoming traffic then go down a small ditch, from what she could make out in the dim remaining light.

"Get ready," he called out.

She shook her head, her eyes wide and mouth dried up like she'd eaten cotton.

"I'm sorry! Hang on." Lucas checked for other cars then steered the runaway vehicle across the road and into the low shrubs. As soon as the tires hit gravel and plowed into the bushes, the speed reduced. They bumped and bounced over the rough ground and grass.

Then they entered the water, and the *shhhh* of the tires slamming into a deep puddle filled the vehicle. Moments later, they *sloshed* to a stop.

Lucas hit the radio and called in the incident then tapped the dome light on.

Brielle leaned forward to rest her forehead on the dashboard. "What just happened?"

"We took a course in driving safety that we didn't sign up for."

She turned her head sideways to look at him. "I've never had that happen."

"Me either. Only in the police academy during training."

She slowly straightened her back and looked around. The disturbed water *slapped* against the tires like tiny waves. "Do you think…"

"Yes, I do. Someone must've tampered with these brakes. Probably poked a tiny hole to create a slow leak. This isn't an official police car, and it's old, so it doesn't have the safety mechanisms in place to stop someone from popping the hood and piercing the brake lines."

"But how did they do it at the hospital? Aren't there cameras?"

His jaw ticked. "I have a feeling this happened before that."

A thought struck like an electrical shock. "Lucas, what if we'd been leaving the Gaineses' place? Going down that driveway would've…"

The dim interior couldn't hide the grim expression on his face. "It would've taken us right over the side of Raven's Peak Mountain. To our deaths."

TWELVE

Lucas had just settled at the kitchen table with his Bible and two cups of coffee when Brielle padded in wearing his mom's fuzzy pink robe paired with zebra socks.

Seeing her first thing in the morning—fresh-scrubbed smooth skin, damp hair and a soft smile—caused his rib cage to strangle his lungs. "How'd you sleep?"

She plunked down beside him and set her chin in her palm. "You know that dream where you're falling, and then you jerk awake before you hit the ground?"

He frowned, then nodded.

"That's no fun when it's happening in a car, either."

"I'm sorry. Last night was scary." He twisted his mouth, hating what he had to say next. "Which brings me to something I've been pondering since I woke up. I don't think it's a good idea that you go to the fair with Gabe today."

She straightened in the seat. "Please don't tell me that. I already said I would."

"Blame me, okay? Tell him Uncle Lucas said no." He handed her the second cup of coffee as a peace offering, but she shook her head. "Brielle. Think about what happened last night."

"I know, and I do, but I thought when you and that other officer…?"

"Chris Anders."

"You said it looked like someone had punctured the brake line or something a couple days ago? That it was a slow leak."

"That's true," he admitted. Likely it had been Theodore Hardwick messing with the car the day he interviewed Peter Gaines. Possibly before he attacked Brielle in the basement.

"And hospital cameras confirmed that. No one had loitered around the car at Tunnel Creek General."

"I know where you're going with this." He closed his Bible and sat back.

"We know it was probably Theodore Hardwick who messed with the car. And you said he's going into surgery at the hospital."

"He is, but there may be other players in this. And I don't want to risk you being hurt again."

"Lucas. Please. Don't give me that stubborn look." Her brows shot up. "Hey, what if you come along? The two of us can take Gabe to the fair. It's only twenty minutes outside Tunnel Creek. We'll get him a funnel cake, ride a few rides, maybe do the hedge maze. He's been begging me to do that one since he read about a knight lost in a maze in one of his chapter books. Then when the warrant comes through, you can drop us off and go."

Lucas sighed in defeat. Why was it so difficult saying no to this woman? He grumbled under his breath. "Fine. One hour at the fair. That's it."

"Thank you." She leaned across the table and kissed his cheek, then drew back in surprise. "Sorry."

Don't be, he didn't say. The light kiss had the effect of two large cups of coffee. He just hoped the heat climbing his neck wasn't too obvious. "Let's get going."

Forty-five minutes later she, Lucas, and Gabe drove through the wide gates welcoming visitors to the Oconee County Fair in Noah's oversize truck. Huge white tents, a colorful, towering Ferris wheel, and a swarm of people covered every inch of the property. In the distance, a large gray barn stood out against the bright blue sky.

"We're here." Lucas parked Noah's truck near the edge of the crammed field-turned-parking-lot, and they climbed out of the massive vehicle.

"Mmm. Smell that fair smell." Brielle sniffed loudly.

"Dirty-pig-flavored cotton candy?" Lucas quipped. "My favorite."

"Hey, it could be Wilbur." She sent an elbow his way, then clasped Gabe's hand. "We should be on the lookout for a spider on its web up in the corner above one of the pigs."

"No, please. Not that." Lucas rubbed a knuckle under his eye like he was wiping tears. "That story slayed me when I was a kid." His arm brushed hers as they walked toward the ticket booth. "I kept asking my mom if Charlotte was just hibernating."

"Aw, I'm sorry. It is such a sweet, sad story."

"Which story?" Gabe asked.

"*Charlotte's Web*. Have you read it?" Brielle asked.

"Mommy Kinsley read it to me. I didn't like it." Gabe huffed.

Lucas sent Brielle an *I told you so* look over Gabe's head. He couldn't see her eyes through the sunglasses, but her expression radiated sympathy.

"Isn't it neat how stories stay with us forever?" She asked Gabe. "*Charlotte's Web* was sad, but I was so glad that Charlotte's babies were there to keep Wilbur company and comfort him during his sadness. They reminded him of her." Her words and demeanor softened. "Charlotte's babies were Wilbur's family. Just like ours."

"Yeah, 'cept we're not spiders." Gabe perked up, and Brielle wrangled him into a quick hug.

"Speaking of books." Lucas cleared his throat as they

settled into line. He glanced around, getting his bearings in the crowd. "I still have your early birthday present. It's at Jasper's cabin now. I guess he took it out of his squad car."

"The book that saved me?"

He chuckled. "Yes, that one."

"I've thought of it, but stuff just kept coming up and I'd forget to ask."

"I'll get it to you one of these days." His phone buzzed, and he pulled it out. "Looks like Theodore Hardwick is out of surgery and recovering in ICU."

Brielle's mouth pinched shut and she shook her head, then looked down at her sandals.

"I get it." He leaned over, whispering, "Pray for justice, okay?"

"Yes. Justice."

Still, even with the man who'd come after Brielle completely incapacitated and the end of this case in sight, he couldn't let his guard down. Something told him this storm wasn't over yet.

After they bought their tickets, she, Lucas, and Gabe set off into the fray. Brielle tried not to notice the fact that Lucas still seemed unsettled, or that she was getting way too used to having him around every day.

"What's going on in that mind of yours?" He asked as Gabe threw fistfuls of fish food into a pond teeming with beautiful, spoiled koi.

She met his eyes beneath the transition lens glasses and offered a playful shrug. Like she was going to tell him her thoughts or feelings, especially about him. Lucas had made it clear all those years ago he only viewed her as Jasper's sister. A little sister to him as well. He cared about her but not in *that* way.

"I'm trying to enjoy the moment." She clung to Gabe's

arm as she led him to the handwash station. "Usually, I'm here manning a booth and can't walk around much. By the way, thanks again for paying. You didn't have to do that."

"I wanted to."

She'd been prepared to pay for him and Gabe but appreciated Lucas taking care of them. He waved it off when she asked if he would join them on the rides, too.

"I'll be your fixed point on the ground." Then he gazed solemnly at her, and Brielle's stomach swooped like she was already on the Tilt-A-Whirl ride.

Stop it, Brielle. Because when Lucas's teasing words from that day at the lake all those years ago came back, the hurt returned, too. And the rejection.

I was wondering if you wanted to go to homecoming next year.

Homecoming? He'd looked confused. *That's three months away. It's still summer.*

I'm a planner, she'd admitted with a shrug, curling her toes into her rubber flip-flops.

You're serious?

He'd looked straight at her finally, wearing a bewildered expression.

How she'd wished to dive into the water and sink below the surface right then. But she wouldn't back down now. *Yes.*

You're Jasper's little sister. He'd kill me. Plus...

He'd stared out at the water just then, a dreamy expression in his eyes. *I'm going to ask Leah Parner to homecoming.*

And that was that. Lucas had drawn a line in the sand. Back then, she talked herself out of her disappointment by reminding herself he was three years older. She was an underclassman. Also, Jasper's sister.

Brielle shook off the unwelcome memory and focused

on Gabe. "What would you like to do next?" she asked her nephew. The June sun beat down on them, and the lowing of a cow carried over from the barn. "Rides, food, or see the animals."

"Animals. Please, Auntie Bee." Gabe looked up at her, his bowtie upper lip crinkled and his freckles highlighted on his cheeks. Now this, this was love. And oh, how she loved this little man.

Her infatuation with Lucas would dim. *Eventually.*

"Then animals we shall see." She curled her arm over his shoulder and guided him in a semicircle until they changed direction and headed toward the barn, where 4H groups judged everything from pigs to chickens to cows to the funniest-looking bunnies she'd ever seen.

Thirty minutes later, she and Lucas emerged from the barn, Gabe atop Lucas's broad shoulders, his small hands holding Lucas's head like it was a big round steering wheel.

Lucas clasped his arms over Gabe's little legs and sent Brielle a grin she memorized.

"I had no idea there were one thousand, six hundred and forty-three types of chickens." Lucas dipped his head close to hers. At least he seemed more relaxed now.

"There were a lot." She looked up at Gabe. "Which chicken was your favorite?"

"I like them *all.*" He drew out the word. "What one did you like, Auntie Bee?"

"The cotton ball chicken was the coolest."

"He's a silkie chicken," Gabe corrected.

"You're as smart as your mom. She would remember all those chickens, too. Hey, I was thinking we could get some fair food next. What are you two guys in the mood for? Chocolate, ice cream, popcorn, or a funnel cake?"

"I want it all," Lucas declared, rubbing his flat stomach.

"You will make your stomach throw up, then," Gabe answered matter-of-factly. "I did that once when Daddy let me make an ice cream sundae then I ate my own popcorn then he fell asleep and I threw up." He pulled a sick face, sticking out his tongue.

Ten minutes later, they sat on a bench with treats. Gabe held his ice cream cone, Brielle a plate with a partially eaten funnel cake, and Lucas shoveled buttered popcorn from a white bag into his mouth, his expression and body language distant again. Was he upset about paying again? She'd offered but he'd insisted on paying. What was wrong? They finished their drinks, then stood.

"Hey, are you okay?" she asked Lucas. "I could've paid back there—"

"No, it's not that." His phone beeped. "Just a sec." He replayed the voice mail in text, then released a frustrated sigh. "The company that sold the security system to the Gaineses called. They're claiming the footage at the mansion isn't viewable. I'm wondering if the most recent footage was purposely damaged."

"I'm sorry." She hesitated. "Is that why you're upset?"

Lucas tucked away his phone and stared off in the distance.

"Yes, and no. It's not just the case. This place, even the food, brings back memories. Complicated ones, you know?" He rubbed a hand across his mouth. "We came here once. Leah liked the funnel cakes, too." He shook his head. "I don't mean to be a downer."

Hurt pooled in her chest, but she squared her shoulders. "We can leave if you'd like? Or I can take Gabe on a ride while you call the security camera company back?" Brielle transferred her attention to Gabe. "How about the hedge maze, Gabe? I heard this year's maze is extra high because of all the rain this spring."

"Yes!" He bounced up and down, and they trotted over

to the maze entrance, where a group of teens exited with rowdy shouts of who finished first and who got lost and who cheated.

Lucas followed, then came up beside them to peer at the entrance, which was split in half and had a sign over it that said *entrance* on the right and *exit* on the left. "You have your cell?"

She nodded, plucking the strap of the small cross-body purse she wore today. Her cell was inside.

"Come on, Gabe. We'll go through and see how fast we can make it." She pointed at the sign beside the maze. "Look, the record is four minutes and thirty seconds. Set last year. Think we can beat it?"

He nodded fast, and then they set off. Brielle didn't look at Lucas as they hurried toward the maze. He suddenly reached out, clasping her wrist as they brushed by each other. "Call if anything strange happens. Anything. I'll be right here."

Not for much longer.

The thrill of having Lucas Scott care was erased by the realization she was a victim of a crime he was trying to solve. To him she was Leah, except she'd survived.

"We'll be fine." She pulled away and led Gabe to the entrance portion of the maze. And she didn't look back.

They entered the maze, and instantly her senses heightened as the thick hedge cut off the raucous sounds of fairgoers on rides and the boisterous crowds that dotted the fairgrounds. Foot traffic packed the dirt ground, silencing their steps as they wound around one corner and considered the next two choices.

"Left or right?" she asked Gabe as she pushed back the irrational hurt from Lucas's comment about Leah. He still loved her. That much was clear.

"This way." Gabe pointed right and they trotted around

the right turn and into another section of the maze. A teenage couple passed them, giggling and holding hands. Her mind betrayed her, returning to the summer she embarrassed herself in front of Lucas.

Drop it. He probably didn't even remember.

They weaved around another pair of identical corners. Was he still on the call?

"Auntie Bee, where do we go now?"

Suddenly they found themselves at a dead-end. "Oops, looks like that was the wrong way." This corner of the maze was almost eerily silent. Must be the back side. She turned in a circle and squinted at the hedge.

"Did we make it to the end?" Gabe asked.

"No, the end is near the beginning part. Where we walked in, but on the other side of it." This looked like a back corner. "This part is a dead-end."

"*Dead*? Why's it dead?"

"That's just the name when you can't go anywhere else and have to turn around." She snagged his hand and turned him around, only to find a petite man wearing a black hoodie standing in the spot they needed to go to, the hood pulled over his head and large, dark sunglasses covering half of his face.

Brielle's heart gave a little lurch, and she slipped her hand into her small purse. Where was her cell? She groped for it as her pulse kicked up. It was probably just a Goth teenager, lost just like they were.

No, this looked like a middle-aged man, considering the thicker midsection beneath the hoodie and the dark blond mustache.

She positioned Gabe at her side, farther away from the stranger, then took tentative steps to get around the man. Her muscles quivered with each stride. She veered so far around him her arms brushed the sharp, prickly branches of the hedge as they passed. Why was he looking at her like that?

At the last moment, the man reached into his pocket. Was he getting a gun?

Brielle screamed and pushed Gabe forward.

"Run, Gabe!" She staggered after him, but the man grabbed her arm.

"Come with me or the kid gets hurt," he growled in a strange voice.

Brielle screamed again and writhed away from the man's grasp. Something sharp stabbed her wrist. She cried out. Gabe dashed away, running ahead of her. Then he turned and shouted.

"Auntie Bee!"

"Go, Gabe, run!" The man tried to wrap his arm around her, and his other hand pulled out a gun. *No!* She ducked, slammed her foot down on his, and scuttled backward. Her purse collided with the gun and loosened it enough that the weapon fell onto the maze's dirt path.

The attacker dove for it. Brielle was torn. Fight to get the gun or run after Gabe?

Run.

She sprinted after Gabe, who had turned a corner and disappeared from view. Desperation choked her. What if the man caught up? Was this Peter Gaines? Where was Gabe? Brielle looked at the ground. That was no help. An army's worth of footprints littered the earth, and his fresh, smaller ones were nearly impossible to separate from the others.

"Lucas!" she shouted as she ran. "Gabe! Gabe, where are you?"

She came upon a long row and didn't recognize it; in fact, she was sure she hadn't been this way yet. Her heart double-timed as she checked behind her.

If only the hedge weren't so high.

"Lord, help me, please." Tears stung her eyes. The sound of footsteps—adult-sized footsteps—coming her way from the other side made her break into a run. She took off in the opposite direction, turning another corner. Then ran smack into a large, tattooed man. The heavyset woman beside him shrieked as the man caught her with one burly arm.

"Hey, lady, what is wrong with you? Slow down."

"There's a man back there." She panted, trying to speak. "Black hoodie, sunglasses. He—he came after me and my nephew." A sob worked up her throat. "Have you seen a little boy with a blue shirt and jean shorts? Light brown hair?"

They gaped at her, then the blonde woman stepped forward. "I did see a little boy run past us, back there." She pointed behind them, her bracelets jangling. "To the right, I think. Oh, I can't keep this straight. What did the man look like who came after you?"

"I'm sorry, I have to find my nephew." Brielle dashed around them and took the direction the woman said. She came to yet another turn that looked the same and cried out. Which way?

"Gabe! Answer me." The sob rose from the depths of her soul. She had to protect him. "Where are you?"

"Auntie Bee?"

His tiny voice broke through her despair.

Another sound carried over, too, this one a faraway siren-like noise. She ignored it and listened for Gabe's voice.

"Keep talking, Gabe. I'm almost there."

"Is the bad guy there?"

"No, it's just me. Tell me where you are, Gabe."

"I'm in the bushes."

Me, too. He must be on the other side of the hedge. But how could she get to him? She clawed at the thick shrub, crying and shouting. Breaking branches and grabbing clumps of leaves. Brambles poked her skin and pain skittered across her wrist.

"Brielle!" Lucas's voice.

She almost collapsed as her muscles went limp. *Thank You, Lord.*

"Where are you?" he cried.

"I'm here." She answered, then let out a frustrated moan. How could she describe it to him?

"Just keep talking to me." He was nearly shouting.

"I'm sorry, I should've waited for you."

"And I should've come with you."

"Lucas?" The hedge wiggled slightly, and she pushed her arm through.

"I'm here. I have Gabe." A pause. "We're on the other side of the hedge. Are you alone?"

"Yes." No sign of the man who'd come after them.

"Hold on."

She held as still as she could with her body shaking wildly. Suddenly the branches in the hedge shook and trembled even more, and pieces dropped away. How was he doing that? Finally, his arm appeared, then both arms. Red scratches marked up his skin.

"Lucas." She crouched on unsteady legs to reach the stomach-level opening. His eyes met hers, and he gave her a half smile.

"Found you."

She'd never been so happy to see someone. He reached through and she did, too, clasping her hand to his. They twined their fingers, and she inhaled a shallow breath then glanced behind her. The heavyset young couple she'd run into came up behind her.

"Who are you?" the tattooed man demanded, leaning down to glare at Lucas. "This lady is in trouble. I saw a guy in a black hoodie run past a minute ago. Tried to stop him and he kicked me and got away."

"This is Lucas Scott. He's a CSI agent," Brielle volunteered in a shaky voice. "He's my…my friend." And more, but she wouldn't think of that now. Gabe was safe. "He has my nephew. We just need to get to each other."

Lucas readjusted their hands, and their eyes connected again. Holding on tight.

"Don't let go. Please."

"I'm right here. I won't leave."

"I tried…to get away. Stepped on his foot really hard and ran. But it was so confusing inside this. Don't…leave." She didn't care that her voice wobbled or that she pleaded with him. She just knew even though she was safe at the moment, she was in more trouble than she'd ever been.

Because in the midst of this terrifying and trying week, she'd fallen back in love with Lucas Scott.

THIRTEEN

Lucas waved goodbye to Noah and his fiancée, Lucy. They were staying at Jasper's house while Kinsley and Jasper remained in the hospital, since it was easier on Gabe to be at home. Brielle stood beside them, one hand on Gabe's head as the boy waved wildly at Lucas. Trek, the Holts' retired K9 deputy, sniffed the air from the yard, his tail wagging at the commotion.

He'd left Noah's truck and now drove Jasper's squad car, which had been okayed by Chief McCoy when he was apprised of the situation and the cold hard fact that someone else was working with Theodore Hardwick, aka, the Backyard Bandit. And that someone must've damaged the security footage at the mansion on purpose.

Brielle wasn't happy about being left behind, but he wouldn't risk putting her in harm's way again while he and another officer searched the Gaines mansion.

After Brielle gave her statement to an Oconee County deputy on duty at the fairgrounds, she and Lucas had pumped Gabe full with a hot dog and flavored ice, then gotten in the truck and headed home. Brielle had said very little on the ride, and Lucas couldn't stop his brain from replaying her frantic cries in the maze. How desperate he felt when he knew she was in trouble, and yet again, he'd let a woman down he…

Loved? He ground his jaw as he watched Brielle and Gabe go inside, then he pulled away from Jasper's house.

Did he love her? He'd always cared for Brielle like a sister, but his feelings no longer registered on the sibling level. Not at all. Now he found he couldn't be in the same room with her without being consumed by thoughts of her. Without making sure she was okay. Without attempting to make her smile. Being near her.

No, what he felt for Brielle Holt couldn't be just *care*. And he couldn't deny it anymore.

He stewed over this startling realization as he drove back to the Gaines mansion. Lucas guided the car up the winding driveway, attempting to get his mind back on the task. His phone buzzed, and he swiped it. "Agent Scott here."

"Yes, hello. This is Marcia Rush, from the medical examiner's office. We have the information you asked for about Ronald Gaines."

Finally. "Great, go ahead."

"Mr. Gaines was cremated on May 29, following his autopsy. Dr. Haney said the procedure showed that he died of heart failure brought on by a severe ventricular arrhythmia."

"So there was no physical trauma?"

"Um, let me see." A pause. "No trauma."

"Was Mr. Gaines on any medication?"

"Yes." The woman read off several medications.

"Would it be possible to put those in an email?" He shared his email address, then thanked her and hung up. Multiple medications. Huh.

Lucas frowned as he crested the driveway. The massive house came into view, and he drove slowly past it, his mind on what happened at the fair. His unfortunate comment about Leah. Why had he brought her up? He put the car in Park and set his head against the headrest. He couldn't stop picturing Brielle on the other side of that hedge. Her long, tangled hair and frightened eyes. The feeling of panic at being separated from her.

Had Peter Gaines really followed them there and gone after her?

He scowled as he considered the huge house before him and the details of this investigation. Ronald Gaines had owned a construction company for many years. Several years ago, he passed that ownership on to Peter. Peter in turn lost a large amount of money through failed business deals and broken contracts. However, Ronald Gaines owned this home outright and everything in it. Plus, he had some stocks and other accounts. Despite some financial setbacks, Ronald Gaines had died a wealthy man.

Then there was Stella. She must've known Peter lost some of their father's money. Could there be friction between the siblings because of that? Did she think Peter's mishandling of the family business caused stress for their father, which in turn caused his death?

He exited the car and started toward the front doors. Passing under the stone arch doorway, Lucas noted the tiny white camera in the corner to the left of the doors as he rang the doorbell.

A woman answered, her short, spiky hair and diminutive frame identifying her as Stella Gaines. This should be interesting. "Yes, what do you want?"

"Ms. Gaines?"

"I'm Stella Gaines. Who are you?" She squinted and held onto the door like she might fall over if she let go.

"Agent Lucas Scott with South Carolina Law Enforcement Department." Lucas revealed the single piece of paper signed by the judge. "I have a warrant to search the premises. Where is Aidan Donaldson?"

"Search the house? Why?" Her large brown eyes seemed to take over her face.

"TCPD is working an active investigation. Occupants in this house may be connected to the case."

"Are you kidding me?" Her hand jutted out as she spoke. "My father just died and you police officers want to go through his things?"

"They're Peter's things now, correct?" Lucas used ammunition to see her reaction.

Stella closed her eyes, her mouth tipping down. "It doesn't matter who owns them. Father is dead." She sniffled and turned away but continued speaking. "Aidan stays above the garage in the guest quarters when he graces us with his presence." She motioned across the front of the house. "I can call him if you want."

"He hasn't answered my calls," Lucas noted.

"He's been busy. The last time I saw him he was in the basement going through my father's things with Peter. They were arguing about the stupid fossils. Maybe he left his phone in his apartment when you called."

She motioned him inside and hobbled toward the hallway leading to the kitchen. Her fluffy leopard-print slippers scraped the tile as she walked. "I heard you caught the man breaking in through people's back doors. Good riddance, I say."

"I can't really comment on the case. If you don't mind me asking, where is Peter?" Lucas eyed the expensive-looking decorations and the mirrored ceiling in the dining room.

"I don't know. I'm not my brother's keeper."

They might not like each other, but Peter and Stella Gaines were quite similar in temperament. *Difficult* temperament.

"Is he here at the mansion or somewhere else?" Lucas clarified as they approached a brown door he was almost certain had led him to Brielle the other day when she was being attacked. The basement?

Stella Gaines eyed him, then turned and pointed to the door. "I think Peter went into town today for something. Like I said, I don't know. This takes you to the basement."

"Please stay nearby so I can ask you some questions when we're done."

"I'm not going anywhere, officer. This is my house." She gave a caustic laugh, bunching up the bags under her eyes. "Unless my brother kicks me out."

He waited until Stella shuffled away then started down the stairs. Was she suffering through one of the migraines Mr. Donaldson had mentioned during his interview? If so, he'd give her grace about her foul mood.

He descended the stairs and hit the landing, still pondering Stella Gaines's bitter words and the incongruity of this wealthy, splintered family. They were a sad example that having money, a big house, luxury cars, and nice things didn't provide peace or contentment.

Only the Lord could, he'd learned.

He picked his way past the bookshelves, couches, and the pool table, his gaze roving over the tidy space. A light shone from the second door at the end of the room.

"Mr. Donaldson?"

No answer. Maybe he'd gone back to his apartment above the garage. Lucas shrugged. Might as well take a look while he was here.

Lucas slowed as he passed by the impressive dinosaur fossil collection. He continued on, and when he reached the lit, mostly closed second door, he leaned forward to peek inside. The cracked door revealed blank computer screens and a small desk lamp on, but the rest of the room remained dark.

"Mr. Donaldson?"

Lucas switched on the overhead light then used two fingers to push open the door.

His chest compressed like it was held in a vise.

Aidan Donaldson was slumped in the chair, his head and long torso draped over the desk, arms spread on either side. Drying blood pooled beneath his temple and a small black gun lay under his left palm.

Brielle drew in a slow, shuddered breath as Noah drove her into the Tunnel Creek police station lot. Four words had been chasing themselves around her head on the way into town with her pensive middle brother.

Aidan Donaldson was dead.

Noah helped her out of the big truck, then they strode up to the police station's front doors. He stayed close, his gaze spanning the parking lot.

Was Lucas here, at the station? Or was he still at the Gaines estate, working the scene?

She shuddered even as she longed to see him.

Noah nodded hello to Debra, the receptionist, and Brielle waved, then they headed toward Jasper's office. Brielle stopped in the doorway. Lucas sat at Jasper's desk, a pencil stuck behind his ear as he stared intently at the computer screen.

"Hey, man," Noah said.

"Brielle." Lucas paused. "Noah. Thanks for bringing her in."

Their eyes met across the room, and Brielle willed her cheeks not to flush at his intense perusal.

"Not a problem. Sounds like a rough afternoon."

"I was definitely not expecting what I found." Lucas stood and motioned for Brielle to sit, then pointed at the folding chair for Noah. "Have a seat?"

Noah waved him off. "I'm heading out soon. My mom,

Lucy, and Gabe are back at the house. Jasper and Kinsley may stay another night at the hospital."

"Everything okay with the baby?" Lucas asked.

"Yes, her bilirubin levels are better. Jasper said the doctors just want them at normal levels before they get to go home. And…" Noah paused. "I think with all that's happening, it's not necessarily a bad thing to stay away another night." He dropped his heavy-lidded gaze to Brielle, and again she felt the seriousness and weight of this investigation.

"You might be right." Lucas rubbed the back of his neck.

"Any news about Peter Gaines?" Noah asked.

"Nothing new. There's an APB out, and he's been notified to report to the station when he's back in Tunnel Creek."

Noah leaned over Brielle. "You okay if I head out?"

"Yes. Thanks, Noah."

He said goodbye and headed down the hall.

Lucas returned to Jasper's chair and dropped hard into it. "You heard Mr. Donaldson is dead?"

"Noah told me. I'm sorry you had to…find that."

"It's part of my job. But it's definitely taken this case in an unexpected direction."

She hated to ask, but couldn't help it. "Did Mr. Donaldson take his own life?"

Lucas pulled off his glasses and set them on the desk, and she was immediately reminded of the moment she'd taken them off and looked at him at Jasper and Kinsley's cabin.

"It appears the scene was set up to look that way, but I don't believe he killed himself." He rubbed his eyes, and she noted the shadows underneath and the weariness lining his handsome face. The poor man probably hadn't slept well in days.

"Why don't you think so?"

"A number of things." He replaced his glasses. "Aidan Donaldson was right-handed. The gun was in his left hand. The blood-spatter pattern and body position aren't consistent with a suicide."

She tried not to recoil as she pictured it.

"I'm sorry—you don't need to know those details. So far it appears only Donaldson's prints are on the gun, but that can be done easily. Gloves, positioning."

"Was Mr. Donaldson at the mansion alone? Any sign of Peter?"

"No. Peter's cell phone is going straight to voice mail. As I told Noah, we've put out an APB for him. It sounds like Peter was there overnight, as was Stella, and Peter left in the morning sometime. At least, Stella said she believed her brother was there. She answered the door when I arrived and seemed rather…out of it. She said Peter had gone into town, but as of right now, we can't locate him."

Brielle pictured the brother and sister she'd interrupted days ago. "What if Stella Gaines is behind all this?"

"I've considered that as well. So far there are no connections between Stella and Theodore Hardwick. She has airtight alibis for the situations that have occurred this week, and she also appears incredibly frail and in deep mourning for her father. Mr. Donaldson shared with us during the interview that Stella suffers from migraines and stays inside a lot. She had quite a breakdown after I found Mr. Donaldson."

Brielle nodded slowly. "But she gave her statement?"

"More or less, yes." Lucas pinned her with a hesitant expression. "Before I forget. This is for you." He pulled out a wrapped gift from a desk drawer. "Jasper actually left it here. Happy early birthday."

"Aw, the infamous birthday book. Thank you." She accepted the gift, the solid shape identifying it as a medium-length, hardback book. After all they'd been through, opening the present felt too personal and private, and she wasn't sure she wanted to here at the station. "Do you want me to open it now?"

"Up to you." He shrugged, his nonchalance stinging a bit. "I do have some good news. The hospital called earlier. Shonda has woken up."

Brielle clutched the gift book to her chest. "She has? Can I go see her?"

"I'd like to give her time to come to, let the doctors monitor her. Make sure her vitals are stable before we attempt to talk to her or stress her out."

"She's my friend, Lucas. Does she know what happened?" She turned the gift book over in her lap. "I want to make sure she knows that man is caught."

"I understand, but I don't want to stress her out. Lord willing, there's no memory loss, and she can give her statement soon. Maybe there's additional information she knows that can provide key evidence in the case."

She gave a reluctant nod. "Also, I spoke to a couple of my customers earlier, they inquired if The Antique Depot was open or when it would reopen. I'm wondering about next week?"

Lucas started shaking his head as she spoke, and she squeezed the gift until the wrapping crinkled in her grasp.

"Brielle, I know you want to be done with this situation. As do I, so—"

"So you can go back to your life in Myrtle Beach and leave Tunnel Creek. I know."

"Hold up. What?"

"You want to get home. To Myrtle Beach." She fought to keep the hurt from her tone.

"Well, yes." He drew out the word. "But also so *you*

can get back to your store and *your* life." His brows drew together in a sharp V. "I…care about you. A great deal, in fact." He swallowed. "I need to know you're…*safe*. Don't you want that?"

"Yes. Of course, I do." Her heart hiccupped. But that wasn't all she wanted.

She wanted Lucas.

Once again, her feelings toward this serious, soft-hearted man rose to the surface. Only this time she wasn't fifteen, with star-crossed eyes and homework assignments due. This time, her heart was fully his, but she was pretty sure he wasn't interested.

Lucas leaned back in Jasper's chair, squinting at the sunlight pouring through the blinds. It was nearly ten a.m. He'd gotten Brielle's statement last night then taken her back to Jasper's cabin with two large pizzas in tow. She'd been quiet and withdrawn, responding to his questions with single-word answers. Had he said something to upset her? Or was it because he hadn't allowed her to visit Shonda yet?

Or…was it something more? About them?

Hope flared in his chest. Could it be that she, too, realized once this case was solved, he would have no reason to stay. He'd never wanted to solve a case more, and yet… he wasn't sure he'd ever be ready to leave her.

He'd gotten used to her being close by. Used to their conversations. Used to her smiles and their teasing each other about books.

"Focus, Scott."

Lucas opened the email from the ME again. Ronald Gaines had been on two heart medications, one blood thinner, furosemide for edema, and a blood pressure medication. Which family member had kept track of his medications, making sure Ronald took them exactly when he was supposed to? The medical examiner said they had the medications for pickup in case an officer needed to see them.

He'd stop by there when he left the station.

Lucas moved on to something else. He'd searched multiple databases to find anything else he could about Ronald Gaines and his family. Their history. Peter had been divorced once and Stella twice.

A byline from forty years ago snagged his attention. *Faded Hollywood Star Dies in a Car Accident, Leaving Daughter to East Coast, Millionaire Father.*

His phone chimed. He growled and grabbed it, squinting at the fine print on the computer screen at the same time. "Scott here."

"We got him." Chris Anders's triumphant voice on the other end of the line sent a jolt through Lucas's weary muscles.

"Peter Gaines is in custody?" He clicked to email himself the newspaper article, then closed the database.

"He is."

"Excellent. Well done." Lucas stood and rushed out into the hall. "Where are you?"

"We're on eighty-four, about five miles outside Tunnel Creek. Mr. Gaines was driving back into town when we caught him. He's refusing to talk until his lawyer arrives. Says he had no idea Aidan Donaldson is dead."

"As expected." Lucas strode out of the office while letting Chris know he'd be stopping at the medical examiner's office then heading out that way. "I'll be there in twenty minutes."

He updated the other officers on the case, then jogged to Jasper's squad car. Six minutes later he pulled up in front of the ME's office building near Tunnel Creek's town center. The brick-fronted mayor's office, DMV, and city offices were all situated nearby, and a large stone fountain and small park area sat opposite them. Children swung on swings and ran around the playground as their parents watched.

Lucas headed to the ME's front door and rang the bell.

A woman answered on an intercom. "May I help you?"

"This is Agent Lucas Scott with SLED. I spoke to Marcia last night. I'm here to pick up Ronald Gaines's medications for an investigation."

"Oh, yes, just one moment, Agent Scott."

She buzzed him inside. The plain brown walls and nondescript furniture reminded him of a seventies sitcom, and the woman who buzzed him in—Marcia, her name tag affirmed—gave him a buttery smile. "I'll be right back with the medications."

As Lucas waited, he pulled up the email he'd sent himself. His eyes narrowed as he read the article. It talked about Ronald Gaines and a woman—an actress—he had an affair with four decades ago…then the actress had died and the wealthy, married builder adopted the child he fathered. A little girl. Wait a minute. Stella Gaines's *mother* was a Hollywood actress? Lucas's jaw went slack. *Stella was Peter's half sister?* Did Peter know? What about Aidan Donaldson? Had both men been protecting the fragile woman from the truth of her birth and adoption?

More importantly, did Stella know this?

"Here you go." The woman appeared in front of him, handing him a small blue sack with white handles.

"Uh, thanks." He slipped his phone in his pocket, then brushed through the pill bottles inside. Lucas looked up. "Didn't you say there were five medications?" He pulled out the four bottles. "Your email said he also took Digoxin for his heart?"

"Those are the only medications his family members surrendered after the paramedics picked up the body."

Marcia's face registered worry and confusion. "I can contact Dr. Haney, but she's not supposed to be available today. Just back from vacation," she explained.

Lucas frowned. "So there's one medication missing, the Digoxin?"

"It appears that way. I'm sorry, I just collected what we have in the back."

"That's okay. Thank you." He turned and strode back to the squad car, a flood of questions circling his mind like water down a drain. Did Stella Gaines know she was a half sister to Peter Gaines, adopted at the age of three?

And where was the bottle of Digoxin?

FOURTEEN

Brielle pulled into her store and parked. Noah had taken her to get her truck from Lucas's parents' condo an hour ago. It felt strange—but nice—to drive herself around again. Had it only been days ago, barely a week, that she'd driven here and ended up nearly getting killed? Now Theodore Hardwick was in custody, along with Peter Gaines.

Pray for justice, Lucas had told her. She prayed they'd never bother her or anyone else again.

And praise God, Shonda was out of the coma and responding to commands. Even trying to talk, Jasper said in a brief phone call. He'd visited Shonda in the hospital right before he and Kinsley checked out and headed back to the cabin with Maggie. Shonda said she wanted to see Brielle, Jasper reported.

Brielle climbed out of her truck and slipped Lucas's book gift under her arm, then trudged up to the front door. The police tape was finally gone, and she punched in the code and entered her store. The last time she'd been here, Lucas was with her, and now the space felt empty and forlorn by herself. Or maybe it was just her feeling that way.

Which was foolish. She was safe now, and she had work to do. Customers to call, orders to complete. Items to tag. For now, the Gaines mansion was off the table, but she had enough other jobs to do to fill her time.

To keep her mind off Lucas. Hopefully.

She weaved around furniture on her way to the register and began tidying up the overturned table from the day of the attack. During the process, she eyed Lucas's gift sitting on the counter, and a sad smile worked at her mouth. She should just open it.

"Not yet." For some reason, the thought of opening it alone—without him—felt like it would bring an end to… to what? To their time together?

Stop it. Brielle crouched then climbed onto her hands and knees. She ran her hand beneath the tight space between the bottom of the desk that held the register and the floor. Most likely, books couldn't fit beneath there, but she wanted to check. Just in case.

She slid her arm farther into the narrow opening, cringing at the crumbs and dust clinging to her skin. She really needed to dust this more often. Her pinky bumped into something hard and plastic. What was that? Adjusting her position and pushing until her shoulder jammed against the wood and the floor, she fumbled for it. Still out of reach. She cupped her fingers around the top of the item, pulling it toward her.

Wait—this wasn't a book. Had a customer left a cell phone and it fell between the cracks, and she'd never heard it ring or found it?

Brielle tugged the phone toward her slowly, then inspected it. Dust clumps covered the screen, and she wiped them away. Her eyes rounded. *Shonda*'s cell phone? What was it doing out here, all the way under the register?

No wonder Lucas and the other officers hadn't found it.

She hit the power button then typed in Shonda's code—her birthday, 1202. The screen lit up, and the red battery warning in the corner showed there was only 10 percent left on the cell. She swiped at the face of it, frowned, and pressed the text icon. The most recent text popped up, from the day before Brielle and Shonda were attacked at the store.

Don't do it, Shonnie. You won't like what happens.

Are you threatening me?

If I have to.

What happened to you? I don't want to turn you in Stell. But you gave me no choice. I can't believe you did this. We may share a mom but I am nothing like you. Turn yourself in or I'll go to Brielle's brother. I will.

Brielle stared at the phone. What was she reading? Was this—did this mean Shonda knew Stella Gaines? And they were…*half-siblings*?

The shocking sound of someone breathing close by caused Brielle to scream and back up. Her hip banged into the counter as her gaze clashed with Stella Gaines's, who was standing between the back storage room and the cash register, a gun aimed at Brielle's chest.

"You…you know Shonda?" Brielle should be afraid. She knew that, but she was so shocked by this revelation she could barely stay upright, let alone think straight.

"We're half sisters. Same mom. Except I got the rich daddy." She laughed, the sound like a hyena's cry. "Small world, right?"

Brielle's thoughts finally centered on what was happening. On the danger she was in. She eyed her purse, laying halfway across the counter. Could she call 911 on Shonda's cell?

"Don't even bother trying anything." Stella scurried around to stand between Brielle and the front door. "I have better aim than Teddy, I promise you that." A Cheshire cat grin spread over her small, round face.

"Teddy, as in Theodore Hardwick?"

"Uh-huh."

"Did your brother or Mr. Donaldson know Teddy?"

"Nope. They never had the pleasure of meeting him. Peter did threaten me that he would have Father cut me off if I married another loser again. Like he had any room to talk. Wasting all our father's money on bad investments, then driving his business into the ground."

"So your brother didn't kill Mr. Donaldson?"

"Look, sweetheart, this isn't a confessional. I'm just here to collect that—" she nudged her chin at the phone in Brielle's hand "—and the pills. And maybe kill you."

Her breath stuttered. "What pills?"

"Don't act dumb. My father's heart medication was in his chest of drawers. And, uh, there are a few missing. You know, because he accidentally took too many a couple weeks ago before we took a walk to the basement." She offered another sly grin that made Brielle's skin crawl. "Teddy thought he was being so smart hiding them in a dresser drawer, but he forgot to tell me. Idiot. And then when I realized you'd taken the furniture he put the bottle in, I could've crowned him." She snickered. "He didn't do a very competent job finding them, now did he?"

"The police searched the furniture and the back room. There's no—"

She bit off the next word. The pills in the gray cabinet in the back room! Lodged at the back of the drawer, beneath the files. Did Shonda get to them first and hide the pills there before she was attacked?

"Ah ha, so you *do* know what I'm talking about." Stella advanced, her eyes narrowed and calculating like a cat stalking a cornered mouse.

Brielle's chest tightened as she stared at the gun. There weren't any weapons or tools within reach. If she ducked, she'd get a couple of seconds before Stella came around the counter. Distraction would have to work for now.

"Why did you kill Mr. Donaldson?"

Stella rolled her eyes. "Naive old man. He got nosy after that interview with the cute cop and decided to check the camera footage *before* I ruined it. Bad move. I walked in on him watching footage of Teddy giving my father a few too many pills that night."

For years, Brielle longed to have her dad back in her life. And this self-indulgent woman killed hers. "Why? Why would you do that?"

"You want to know why? Because *that* house was supposed to be mine. All mine. But Peter lost a bunch of Father's money and suddenly didn't like that deal. Then my brother discovered Teddy and I were involved in some… illegal stuff over in California, and he told my father." Her expression iced over. "Father changed the will last year. The only way I could get *anything* was if father died. And even then I only get fifty percent of his possessions. No house."

"We thought you were truly upset about your father's death, that Peter and Aidan were protecting you because you were so frail."

"I'm an actress, sweetheart." Stella lifted a shoulder in a shrug, then flattened her mouth. "Hollywood spits you out as soon as you have your first wrinkle. And I'm tired of playing second fiddle to my ungrateful, greedy brother. Then Shonda betrays me! I'm like, what is going on with my half-siblings?"

"Shonda knew what you did?"

"She read some of my texts from Teddy the day after my father died." Stella grumbled. "We'd just connected a year ago, when she looked me up on some ancestry page. Stupid. I should've known to be more careful around her. She told me to turn myself in. Like that's happening."

"But Peter came after me yesterday at the fair. He was..." She paused, recognition turning in her mind like a key in a lock. "That was *you* in the maze. Dressed as a man." Brielle noted Stella's long nails. "Your nails jabbed me when we fought over the gun."

"The art of transformation and getting into character is part of being a great actress." Pride lifted her pointy chin.

"So Theodore *is* the Backyard Bandit, then?"

Again, that nonchalant shrug. "What can I say, Teddy was good at breaking and entering. A convenient cover, I'd say."

Movement at the front of her store caught Brielle's attention. A police officer darted across the front window. Brielle looked right back at Stella, but it was too late.

"Who's there?" Stella backed up, her gaze flying from Brielle to the front door. "What's going on? They got Peter! They're not supposed to be here."

Brielle darted out from behind the counter, but Stella came at her fast, shoving at her side and pushing her backward. Pain radiated from Brielle's half-healed knife wound, and she braced herself on the counter with gritted teeth. She looked wildly around, then grabbed Lucas's gift and flung it at Stella. The book struck her in the face, and Stella screamed and flailed, loosening her grip on the gun.

Brielle rammed into Stella, but the woman grabbed her arm and yanked her around. They crashed into each other and rolled along the edge of the cash register countertop, fighting for the gun.

"Police! Put your hands up!" Lucas's voice cut through the ruckus. "Brielle, get down."

Brielle freed herself from Stella's grasp then dove away as Lucas stormed out of the backroom, vaulting the counter. A gunshot exploded in her store, and Brielle cried out. Had she shot Lucas?

Please, God. Brielle peeked around the register table in time to see Lucas kicking away Stella's gun. He clipped a pair of cuffs on Stella's wrists as the woman turned on the tears.

"Officer, I didn't do anything. This woman was attacking me."

"You just shot at me."

"But you were threatening me!"

"Tell that to the judge." Lucas finally turned, looking at Brielle as two more officers burst through the front door, weapons drawn.

"She's cuffed, boys." He stalked over to Brielle and drew her upright. "Are you hurt?"

"No, I'm okay. Are you shot?"

"She missed."

Praise God. "But how did you know? We… I…thought it was Peter."

"The missing medication." He sent a glare at Stella, who was being lifted to her feet by the two officers. "Also, I found an article about Stella's birth mom. And I remembered you saying you stamped on the foot of the masked man in the maze. When I searched the Gaines mansion yesterday, I noticed Stella was hobbling like her foot was hurt."

"Lucas, I noticed a bottle in the gray cabinet when we were here the other day. I assumed the medication was Shonda's, but now I realize it must belong to Ronald Gaines and Shonda hid it there. I'll show you where I found it."

She grabbed the gift book from Lucas and explained what Stella had confessed as he guided her toward the back of the store. The other officers dragged a sobbing Stella outside.

When they were alone in the back room, he turned to her, his features grave. "I'm sorry you had to deal with this alone."

"I wasn't alone. God gave me strength. And He brought you here in time."

He nodded slowly. "Listen, about how we left things earlier. I wanted… There was so much to say, but I'm not good at this. Not good at seeing things that are right in front of me."

Did he mean what she thought he meant?

"Do you see them now?"

"Crystal clear." Lucas folded her into his arms, the wrapped gift book between them. She reveled in his strength and steadiness.

He pulled back, and she held up the book. "I think it's the perfect time to open this." She slit open the wrapping. An ornate, detailed blue cover was revealed, and she gasped. "I shouldn't have thrown this!"

"My mom said one of her favorite stories was *The Blue Castle*, and I found that at an antique store back home. I thought of you."

Her heart clenched. *Back home.* She held in tears as she stroked the beautiful cover. "I love it. I've never read it, but I will now. Thank you."

"Brielle..." He paused, compressed his mouth. "I've been wondering..."

She waited, basking in the warmth of Lucas's intense gaze. "What is it?"

"You asked me something once, and I turned you down."

Did he mean by the lake, all those years ago? Heat climbed her throat, blanching into her cheeks. She tried to pull away, but he held her fast. "Hold on, please. For a few reasons, that wasn't the right time for us. But today...right now, I think it might be."

"The right time for what?" She gazed into his blue eyes, and suddenly he let her hands go and cupped her face.

"For this." His eyes burned into hers, with longing and a question.

She answered with a smile.

Then Lucas pressed his lips to hers, and Brielle forgot about everything else except the man she loved and their bright, book-filled future.

EPILOGUE

Brielle looped her arm through Lucas's as they stepped out of the Biltmore Estate's grand front entrance. They'd driven an hour and a half to visit the estate in all its holiday glory, and Lucas had been a trouper as she peered into every nook and crevice and corner she was allowed to. She'd been here two other times, but this third time? This was special. She wasn't alone or working in the area on a buying trip.

She and Lucas were spending their first Christmas together. His parents were thrilled to have him back in Tunnel Creek, heading up the new crime scene investigative unit in town and serving the other small towns nearby.

Brielle had continued with her antiquing, but traveling the East Coast no longer held the appeal it once had. Leaving meant time away from Gabe, baby Maggie, her mom, her brothers and their wives. And, of course, Lucas.

"How about we go through the garden?" Lucas interrupted her musing.

"Yes, please." A collection of trees decorated with small white lights filled the lawn, and a few people mulled around, sipping hot chocolate.

"Here we are." Lucas opened the stately conservatory's door and led her inside. Instantly, the hush of the warm air and the vibrant pop of flowers flooded her senses. In here, roses still bloomed and life continued.

As it had after her dad's death. Finally, she could see that. While she'd do anything to have him alive and part of their lives, now she fought the grief by giving thanks for her grace-filled Mom and that God had seen them through the difficult years following Dad's death.

They circled the inside once, then Lucas motioned to a black iron bench backed up by a bright wall of red roses. "Would you like to sit on the bench?"

"Sure."

They sank to the cold surface, and he wrapped an arm around her shoulders.

"Do you mind if I take a selfie?" she asked.

"Not at all."

"Hold on, let me get my phone." She unzipped her purse and searched for her cell. A motion next to her diverted her attention.

Lucas was now propped on one knee before her, his palms out and those blue eyes intensely focused on her. Brielle's heart caught in her throat.

"Lucas?"

His gaze traced her face tenderly, then he blinked like he was thinking hard about something. "Brielle, 'I ask you to pass through life at my side—to be my second self, and best earthly companion.'"

She gasped, pressing a hand to her mouth. Was Lucas quoting the garden scene from *Jane Eyre*—and did he mean…?

"You, Brielle, 'I must have you for my own—entirely my own. Will you be mine? Say yes, quickly.'"

"Lucas." She fell to the ground with him, still holding his hands. "You memorized that from *Jane Eyre*." He grinned then, and she wrapped her arms around him.

"Hey, I'm not done yet." He cleared his throat as she pulled back to gaze at him. "I hope you know that I love you. I love your smile and your kindness and your faith. I love our friendship and laughing together. I love that you love books, too. And with God's help, I will do my best to respect, protect, and love you all the days of my life, if you will have me?"

She wiped her tears, her chin quivering. "Lucas." What else could she say?

He reached into his jacket pocket and pulled out a small white box.

Warmth spread through her chest as he tucked his chin and opened the little box. Inside, a beautiful ring glittered in the sparkling white lights. He slipped out the antique, emerald-cut diamond filigree ring and slid it on her left ring finger.

"You went back to get it?" She'd noticed the ring at an antique store in Myrtle Beach when she had driven there with him a few months ago to help him move some of his things.

"I did."

"It's so beautiful. You didn't mind getting an *old* ring?"

"You said you loved it."

"I do. I love *you*." She kissed him. "I suppose my brothers knew about this?"

"I asked their permission, yes. I know it hurts to not have your dad here, but I wanted to honor him by asking them for your hand in marriage."

"Thank you."

Lucas cupped her cheek and gazed at her, then he kissed her again as their future flared brighter than all the Christmas lights in the entire mansion.

* * * * *

If you liked this story from Kerry Johnson,
check out her previous
Love Inspired Suspense books,

Snowstorm Sabotage
Tunnel Creek Ambush
Christmas Forest Ambush

Dear Reader,

Thank you for reading *Hidden Mountain Secrets*! The more time I spent with these characters, the more real and endearing they became. I'll miss the Holt siblings and their loved ones as I begin my next series.

Brielle and Lucas struggle with dangerous secrets uncovered at the Gaines mansion, and they struggle with secrets—and regrets—of their own. Brielle spent her days searching for earthly treasure and lost sight of the real treasure in front of her…her relationship with God and her family. For Lucas, he must forgive himself for what happened to his fiancée in order to step into the future God has for him.

I love connecting with readers! You can find me on my Facebook author page (Kerry Johnson, Author), Instagram (@kerryjohnsonauthor), or on my website, www.kerryjohnsonbooks.com, where you can sign up for my quarterly newsletter. God bless you and keep you!

Fondly,
Kerry Johnson